Author Dedication:
To Melissa Thurgood, the truest person I know.
My bestie by osmosis.

Whisper
published in 2011 by
Hardie Grant Egmont
Ground Floor, Building 1, 658 Church Street
Richmond, Victoria 3121, Australia
www.hardiegrantegmont.com.au

A CIP record for this title is available from the National Library of Australia

Text copyright © 2011 Chrissie Keighery
Design and illustration copyright © 2011 Hardie Grant Egmont

Cover illustration by Emma Leonard
Designed and typeset by Stephanie Spartels

5 7 9 10 8 6
Printed in Australia by McPherson's Printing Group, Maryborough, Victoria, an
accredited ISO AS/NZS 14001 Environmental Management System printer.

The paper this book is printed on is certified against the
Forest Stewardship Council® Standards. FSC® promotes
environmentally responsible, socially beneficial and
economically viable management of the world's forests.

FSC
www.fsc.org
MIX
Paper from
responsible sources
FSC® C001695

Whisper

BY **Chrissie Keighery**

hardie grant EGMONT

chapter 1

Making wishes is for kids – and idiots. I should be able to stop myself, since I'm not a kid anymore. Or an idiot.

But I can't help it. I make wishes, even though it's a bit like bungee jumping. You've got to be crazy to jump off a bridge. Crazy enough to believe that a rubber band will save you even though you are hurtling towards the rocks below.

I've decided I can't keep doing it to myself. So here I am.

I take a deep breath as I get on the tram. Someone stands up to get out at the next stop. I try not to blink as I make my way through the crowd towards that spare seat. There's a wild element to the tram's swaying. A possibility of derailing.

I force the thought out of my head. I will control myself. *Focus.*

I don't realise until I sink into the seat that I've been holding my breath. I breathe out shakily.

My seat faces backwards and it's too far away from the door. But I can't think about it. Maybe if I distract myself by looking at the other passengers I won't freak out.

There are rows of arms reaching up to swaying handles hung from the steel rail. I can see the open pores on an old man's nose. The square of a wallet in a boy's drooping back pocket.

At each stop the tram adds more passengers than it subtracts. Three schoolgirls get on. They look about my age. Their blazers are purple and so are the ribbons in their hair.

One girl's hair reminds me of a horse's mane. It falls in a ponytailed clump, and looks like it would be coarse to the touch. Her face is long too. I imagine how her voice might sound, though her lips are sealed in a no-seats-available pout. Maybe she would whinny? Bray?

She looks me up and down, sees the new uniform I am wearing. She knows where I'm going.

I meet her eyes when they're at the final stages of checking me out. My heartbeat quickens. I look away. I wouldn't have done that before. I would have met that stare, and held it. I would have checked *her* out the same way she's checking me out.

Now I let it go. Anything not to draw attention to myself. Anything not to let the panic take over.

Her friends have their iPods out. I squeeze my eyes shut, blocking out the memories. I loved my iPod. I used to scroll through mine for the perfect song for any given moment.

Unless Nadia has updated it, my music would be completely out of date now. But what do I care?

When I open my eyes again, I'm glad to see the girls have moved down the tram, away from me.

A man in a grey pinstriped suit stands in front of me. The tram's crowded, but I'm not sure he needs to be that close. The fabric of his suit makes contact with my knee and lingers there. I move my legs away sharply.

He looks down at me. The smile he gives is an embarrassed one. It's an apology, and I can see he hopes I know it was just circumstance. That he hadn't meant to be sleazy. His eyebrows lean together and the creases around his eyes soften as his lips mouth sorry.

It's easier to cut through all the crap, all the mixed messages, when people have wrinkles around their eyes. Jules told me that, and he was right as always. It's other teenagers that are the hardest to read.

I feel bad about jerking my knees away. I should have waited, should have read his intentions on his face, in his posture. Jules has taught me well and I'm getting pretty good at it. It must be the nerves.

My phone vibrates. I realise I've been clutching it the whole time, like a lifeline. It's a text from Nadia.

2day is the 1st day of the rest of yr life.
☺ **Good luck xx.**

My throat closes up, even as I roll my eyes. Normally I hate that type of platitude. The smiley face should be enough to make me puke.

But there's nothing to puke. There's a giant, hollow space in my guts and it's not just because I couldn't eat breakfast.

I stare at Nadia's message. I won't delete it. We've been through so much together. She's forgiven me. I think I've forgiven her. I don't think she would ever suspect that she's on my private list of reasons. The list of reasons that led to me being on this tram, going backwards or forwards or wherever the hell I am going.

I text back.

Thnx nads.

It takes me a while, but I add two kisses. And then two more: **xxxx.** She'll be surprised by that. It's almost like the row of kisses is a link between the life I am leaving behind and the unknown ahead.

I have a sudden urge to get up, to jump off the tram and run back. To forget this whole idea. Even though my life was going wrong, at least it was a wrong I knew.

My breathing has become shallow and fast again, but I won't let the panic take control.

It's my stubbornness that keeps me planted. Or maybe it's because Horse Girl and co are blocking the door and I don't trust my legs to get me past them. I want to send my legs a message, to warn them that I need them to be strong.

My phone jumps around in my hand again.

Just be your beautiful self, Demi. And remember, nothing is irreversible xx Mum.

She's good, Mum. She seems to be able to hitch a ride on my doubts even when she's not with me.

The message almost makes me laugh. She's still having a go, even now, after the decision has been made! At least I know where my stubbornness comes from.

I look out the window. I force myself to reply.

Ta mum. I'll be fine.

As my thumb hovers over the send button, I feel flimsy, unsure. I have a silly hope that writing the words might actually make them true. I don't add any kisses. Mum can turn a lifeline into a chain.

I look back at her text. It's not true, what Mum's written – some things *are* irreversible. And there's no point wishing what happened didn't happen.

I learnt that a year and a half ago. When I went deaf.

chapter 2

You never think, when you're fourteen and a half, that something like this might happen. I was sick, sure. It was a terrible flu, yeah, but it was just the flu. Then my temperature went mad.

I lay in my sweat-soaked sheets, too weak to move. My head hurt so much that I couldn't speak, and anyway I was too tired to call out. Why was the sliver of light coming through the gap in the curtains so bright it stung my eyes? When Mum came to check on me, her face was ragged with worry.

I remember lying in the back seat of the car, though I'm not sure how I got there. I remember wondering why my mum, usually such a control freak, was letting me loll around without a seatbelt. But most of all I wondered why the bones in my skull felt like they were pushing on my brain.

Then I was on a stretcher, being wheeled along a corridor. But it was like it was happening to someone else. Like I was watching TV and the patient looked a bit like me. I remember wondering if Dr McDreamy would soon be feeling my forehead. But there was no Dr McDreamy, only an old doctor with a bad comb-over. Before I slipped out of consciousness there was a little surge of disappointment about that.

I dreamt Mum and I were in the car and we were sinking into quicksand. I was struggling to open a door, a window, anything, to get out. But the quicksand was all around and nothing would open. I felt the panic overwhelm me as I realised we would die. While I gasped for air Mum turned around to me in the back seat.

'Calm down, Demi,' she said in her no-nonsense voice. 'We *will* get out.'

But there was no way out and the quicksand was rising.

Then I was free, somehow, flying in the air and breathing again and when I looked down there was a string that led from my body down to Dad, a tiny dot on the ground. It was as though I was a kite he was flying. He pulled me towards him and I landed in the narrow hospital bed.

I was pretty sure I wasn't still dreaming because Flawless was sitting beside me, looking perfect as always. I wanted to ask her where the boys were, my beautiful little nephews. I wanted them there. But just the effort of opening my eyes exhausted me and made my head hurt even more and I fell back asleep.

The next time I woke I'd been turned on my side and there was something being pushed into my spine. A needle, maybe. Dad was holding my hands, as though he were trying to grab hold of my pain, to take it on himself. His eyes were liquid.

I wanted to yell at him to wipe away the tears because dads don't cry. And anyway, I needed to see his eyes properly. I thought they might have the answers to what on earth was going on. But still I couldn't speak. Even his hands holding mine couldn't keep me there, and I drifted away again.

It was five days, Mum told me later. Nearly a week of not knowing if I would survive. My head was still throbbing when I woke up. My neck felt rubbery, like there was no bone in it anymore.

Dr McBaldy and Mum stood at the end of my bed. They were talking without making a sound. I couldn't even hear them whispering. I thought they were being pretty stupid. If they didn't want to wake me, why didn't they talk in the corridor?

Out of the corner of my eye I saw two men in hospital blue racing past the open door, a stretcher between them. I could see their mouths moving. I could see the wheels under the stretcher turning. Shouldn't all that be loud? And where were the beeps of the machines, the other hospital sounds? How was it possible to mute a whole hospital scene? And *why?*

The skirt of my new uniform is navy, criss-crossed with lines of red and grey. Identifying colours. I stand up and sling my backpack over my shoulder. My stop is next. I keep my eyes on the door.

Horse Girl and co get off at my stop. I hang back, wait for them to clear out. But once I'm off the tram we're stuck on the traffic island together. I'm glad the girls don't look back at me. They cross the road when a gap in the traffic appears.

I wait for the green man to tell me when to cross. Cars and motorbikes can appear out of nowhere, and as everyone keeps reminding me, I won't hear them coming.

The three girls move off, sticking their earphones in as they go. They are choosing to block out the sounds of the world. It's a choice I used to make without thinking.

I coach myself on my breathing, trying to calm the nasty doubts that flip around the edges of my mind. I've already decided. It's too late for old doubts to come in and start messing things up.

I watch as the girls reach their school gate. It's only a couple of hundred metres from the gate I'm standing in front of now.

As I walk through the wrought iron gate I feel like I'm passing through a portal. Like everything inside is going to be weird and magical. But the gravel on the other side of the gate just feels like normal gravel.

I walk past a little girl hanging upside down on the monkey bars. Two boys chase each other, one tossing a handful of tanbark at the other's back.

The gravel pathway leads to the office. I walk inside.

The office lady looks busy. She bustles up to the window. I wonder if I should talk or sign.

'I'm new,' I say. 'D-e-m-i V-a-l-e-n-t-i-n-o.' I spell out my name in sign as I speak to cover my bases.

She nods, breathing out through her nose as she does. She checks something on the computer and then points me in the direction of my new homeroom.

I go through the quadrangle. There's a boy sitting alone on a bench. A girl rifling through her school bag. The quadrangle is a large square of green. There are trees and pigeons. It's like they're trying to make the school seem normal, natural. I watch as a flock of birds flies up to the roof.

A red light flashes and spins up there. I know there's no emergency but it still makes me think of ambulances and police cars and disasters.

There's a sudden flurry of students now, summoned by the flashing light.

In the classroom I'm relieved that the desk closest to the door is free. It means that I don't have to walk past anybody.

It also means that I can get out quickly if I have to. I sit down. I keep my head still and let my eyes wander. There are already some kids at their desks, and two more have just walked in. Now there are eight, including me.

At first glance, they don't *look* that different. Not their faces anyway. But there's something kind of overblown, over the top, about the way they're acting. Waving hands everywhere. And their expressions are exaggerated. Not quite right. NQR, as we used to say at my old school.

There's a thump, and I jump as my desk wobbles. When it happens again, I can see the table-thumper is on the other side of the room, near the window. He has bad skin, but good eyes. His eyes are sky blue and fringed by long, dark lashes. He is writing something in his notebook. Then he waves his hand right in front of the blond guy next to him, showing him the note.

That would drive me crazy, such an invasion of personal space. But the blond guy doesn't seem to mind. He reads the note and slowly turns to look out the window. But I think they are both looking at me even though they're pretending to look out the window. I get the distinct feeling that the note is about me and I don't like it.

I give them one of my looks. The don't-mess-with-me. Nadia reckons that look could kill.

The table-thumper looks amused and for a second I

want to point this out to Nadia and roll my eyes. I actually forget that she's not beside me, to point anything out to anymore.

The blond guy gives me an apologetic smile, like he's got the message. It's the second apologetic smile I've got today, and again I feel like I might have misread something. But it's just weird and rude and wrong, teenagers thumping tables and waving their hands like that. I switch my focus to someone else.

There are a few empty seats next to me. Further along there are two girls laughing together. They are signing so fast that it's like their conversation is some kind of race. Their hands swish through the air and I miss most of what they are saying. I get 'hot' and 'boy' before one of them catches me looking. She turns away slightly and I'm blocked out.

There are another three kids sitting in front of me. Two girls and a guy in the middle. I can only see their backs. It's a relief that I can't see their faces and hands. I feel like I'm on overload, that this is all too strange, these people are all too strange.

But as I stare at the guy's back I remind myself I don't have to like it here. I just have to focus and study, so that somehow there might be a future for me after all. There might even be the future I'd planned for, before.

I push that thought away. Another hopeless wish.

Everyone continues what they're doing when the teacher walks in. She's curvy and she's wearing a great dress. It's very sixties, with a geometric print in yellows and blues. She looks like a normal teacher, except prettier.

I notice a pendant thing around her neck. It's the only thing about her that isn't pretty. I think it's a streamer. I saw a brochure about them at one of my millions of appointments with specialists. It explained how a streamer connects someone's hearing aids to their mobile phone or iPod or whatever via Bluetooth.

I feel a stab of jealousy. The teacher must have enough hearing for it to work for her.

The teacher walks to the front of the room, puts her laptop down and stands in front of her desk.

With no warning, she starts drumming her ballet flats on the wooden floor, as though she's in one of those dance movies where it's perfectly normal to break into dance every so often. I feel the vibrations in the soles of my school shoes and give a snort of disbelief. *What the –?*

I was obviously wrong about her seeming normal.

Everyone in class looks up, not like the teacher's off her head, just like she's got their attention.

I realise suddenly that everyone seems too happy for a Monday. Too happy to be at school at the beginning of a new year. And year eleven, when everything matters so much.

I wonder for the millionth time whether I will ever be happy again.

'A big welcome,' the teacher says, with her mouth and her hands, 'to D-e-m-i.'

She finger spells my name, letter by letter. Her thumbs are outstretched, her palms and fingers working in front of her chest.

The other students have gone back to their conversations.

The teacher drums her feet again, and throws her hands in the air. I almost expect her to tap dance across the floorboards. But it's a cue, obviously. My face flushes red as a classroom of hands welcomes me. The three sitting in front welcome me without turning around.

The teacher wags a finger at them, mock disapproval on her face, before she smiles at me. She has a nice smile. Then she turns around and writes her name on the board. Helena. It suits her.

She passes out a timetable to each of us. The school letterhead is printed in bold. The logo is the same as the one on my blazer pocket.

COLLEGE FOR THE DEAF

chapter 3

In hospital there was a competition for the cheeriest smile. It was run by a clown in the children's ward, where I moved after intensive care. The clown started off getting the kids to do a sad face, then a surprised one, then an angry one. Then they had to give their biggest smile.

My new classmates would have won hands down, the way they wear their feelings splashed over their faces.

The clown had stood at the end of my bed, all painted and determined and upbeat.

I didn't win. What on earth was there to be cheery about? I had just been pronounced profoundly deaf.

Profoundly deaf, as in: a piercing scream is like a mosquito buzzing.

As in: I can't hear anyone talk.

As in: stuffed.

I wonder if any of my new classmates lost their hearing the way I did. I doubt it. What happened to me was very rare. Extraordinary. Go me.

Helena stands in front of my desk, patiently, like she's been waiting for me to return from my thoughts for a while.

She taps the desk, the rhythm way slower than my racing heart.

'Do you know where the next class is?' she signs.

I'm relieved her signing is slow and clear. It's taken me a while to get used to the way sign sentences are formed. Often the topic of the sentence is signed at the beginning, so if I miss that, it's hard to work out what's being said. Sometimes I can't work it out at all. Jules taught me how to fill in the gaps but mostly it's just practice.

I shake my head. Helena turns my timetable around so she can read it.

'Follow,' she signs, and nods her head towards the two girls nearby.

She walks over to them. I can't see what they're saying, but the three of them go on for a while. Then Helena stands back so she can see us all and waves us off. I feel like we're being shooed away. I can't imagine any of my old teachers making a gesture like that. It seems kind of rude, like we are cattle being herded around.

But the other girls don't seem to take offence. They just look over at me as they get up and walk out.

I wait a moment, keeping my head down. Slowly, I gather my stuff and head out. The sunshine is bright. I shield my eyes.

Someone smacks my arm.

'I'm E-r-i-c-a,' the smacker says, finger spelling her name.

She must have been waiting for me. It looks as though she's speaking aloud, but she might just be mouthing.

Erica has a cochlear implant, a brown circle of electronic and plastic sticking out of her scalp. I've seen them on people in the audiologist's waiting room.

Mum and I had ridden that hope too. We'd hung on like rodeo riders to the hope that a cochlear implant would change my life back to almost normal. Like a magic trick. But when the audiologist explained how it worked, it didn't seem so magic. They actually take out your own natural cochlear and replace it with the implant.

Whatever sounds or speech come through to you can be kind of robotic. Mum had a really funny look on her face when the audiologist told her about how this version of sound could supersede my *memory* of how things sounded. When she put headphones on mum to let her hear how speech might sound to me if I had a cochlear implant, Mum went all pale, like she was going to faint.

I could see that Mum was freaking out. I could see her thinking that the implant might actually make me seem *less* normal rather than more. And when the audiologist started telling us about the risk of infection from getting a cochlear implant, I decided I couldn't deal with it right then. I had so much to get used to. I couldn't handle any more change.

I couldn't handle any more disappointment if it didn't work out.

Erica's cochlear pushes out of her scalp, quite exposed in her short, browny-blonde hair. It looks weird. Seeing them in the audiologist's waiting room was different. Everyone there was a *patient*. But this girl isn't a patient. She's smiling and chatting and walking around.

If I'd been able to get one, I would have gone for the same dark brown as my hair, and it would have been pretty much hidden. Even though Erica's is exposed and ugly and she really should try and hide it better, I feel a swish of envy.

Erica pulls the other girl over by her hand. She is signing now, not mouthing at all.

'This is ...' Erica is pointing at the other girl and I think she is introducing her but the sign she makes next seems to be 'chatter'. It's her right hand in front of her mouth, thumb below fingers, like a beak opening and closing.

I'm not sure I got it right. Chatter would be a weird name.

'Is that your nickname?' I ask.

'It's not a nickname, it's my deaf name,' Chatter signs back.

Her head is tilted to the side and there's an expression on her face that looks a lot like sympathy because I don't know about deaf names, that I haven't understood.

'You can only be given a deaf name by other deaf people, so it's different. My real name is K-e-i-s-h-a.'

I want to wipe that sympathetic expression off her face. Why would anyone want to have a deaf name anyway? It's not like it's fun or cool or anything to be deaf and have deaf friends. If anyone should feel sympathy here it should be me. At least I *used* to be normal.

I smile tightly at Keisha.

'Sorry about before,' Erica signs. She obviously hasn't noticed my reaction to Keisha. 'Chatter doesn't want ... to know she likes ...'

I don't have a clue what Erica is saying about Chatter or Keisha or whoever she is. Only that she seems to be making the sign for football with her hands while she mouths what looks to be the name Luke.

I try to stomp down on the frustration that's rising inside me. I was missing out on so much at my old school. It's one of the reasons why I decided to go to the deaf school instead. I thought that at least if people were signing and I didn't have to worry about lip-reading all the time, I wouldn't have to deal with only half getting everything.

'Can you please slow down?' I ask and sign, raising my eyebrows to signify a question.

The sign for 'slow down' is one of the first ones Jules taught me. It's like a foot easing off the accelerator pedal, but with the hands instead.

Keisha lightly smacks Erica on the shoulder with the back of her hand and rolls her eyes. It's so *physical*.

'Yes, slow down,' she signs to Erica with a grin.

Keisha doesn't seem to be wearing hearing aids, and I can't see a cochlear implant. I wonder if that means she's as deaf as I am.

'B block is over there,' she points. 'Walk with us?'

I nod.

'Don't you hate English?' Keisha continues, and without waiting for a response goes on, 'it's so crap'.

The sign for 'crap' is like making quote marks with both hands and lowering them quickly. Keisha mouths it as she signs.

I love English – it's my best subject. But I nod as though I agree. It's almost second nature to keep my real thoughts to myself these days. Avoid conflict.

'Who needs a second language?' Erica signs.

She and Keisha laugh. And I feel myself smile, just a little, as I shrug. I've never thought of it like that. But I guess if you've signed all your life, English probably does seem like a second language.

I fall behind the girls. It's not even 9.30, but I'm feeling tired already. I don't even try to keep up with their conversation as we walk down the corridor.

There are noticeboards on the walls. I glance at one with photos as we pass. The next noticeboard is covered with pieces of handwritten work. It's obviously done by kids in the primary school. The writing is messy, the spelling all over the place.

It suddenly makes me think of Harry's note to me. His spelling was also adorably terrible, but the message was clear. That note had floored me.

My parents had been slowly leaking the truth to me.

There were hopes. Meningitis only leads to permanent, profound hearing loss in a small number of sufferers. The hopes rose and fell with each visit to a new specialist. As Mum kept saying, a diagnosis was only an opinion, and an opinion was subjective. There were medical references, the doctors of friends, Google searches. Each would bring up more possibilities.

I attached myself to Mum's hopes. She had always been unstoppable, my mum. She would find a way to lead me out of the silence that suddenly, horribly surrounded me.

When Mum wrote her messages about the next doctor's visit on the pad next to my bed, or on the newly installed whiteboard in the kitchen, Dad often stood behind her, frowning. It was like he had something to say that he thought had to stay unsaid. I sensed he somehow disagreed with what Mum was doing.

Unless you want war, it's best not to disagree with Mum. Dad is a scientist and this is an indisputable fact.

Dad annoyed me then. Actually, he hurt me. I felt like he had given up on me. I couldn't understand it. Dad and I had always been close. We were allies against the united front of Mum and Flawless.

But Dad just stood back with that look on his face as Mum ploughed on. She ploughed on and on until my whole life seemed to revolve around doctors and new tests and different technology. In a way, she's still doing it. But now I know her hopes are hopeless, and her trying to make me normal again is what's annoying.

Thinking back I realise the truth was there, written in the deeply etched lines on Dad's forehead, long before I let myself believe it. As Mum and I trudged off to specialist after specialist, those lines softened and turned into something like acceptance.

But because I didn't want to read those lines, it was Harry, my little nephew, who forced me to face the facts. He was five at the time. He snuck into my room, blond fringe flopping over his eyes. I was reading one of the tacky romance books that Nadia had bought for me, since I'd devoured every decent book in the house. The sticker on the back of the book declared the reduced price of $6.99. The content declared that $6.99 was a rip off.

Harry crept in like a cartoon character, high tip-toed steps to my bedside. He had probably been told not to disturb me. He picked up the notebook and pen from my bedside table. Then he sat in the chair and entwined his skinny little legs around the legs of the chair.

He hadn't been writing for long and his tongue peeked through his lips like it often did when he was concentrating. It took him a few minutes to write his note.

Finally, triumphantly, Harry peeled off the page. He pushed his fringe out of his eyes as he handed the note over.

I Am sore thit Your eyAs dont work. I love you eniwAy.

That all seems like a lifetime ago. But my 'eyas' still don't work, and here I am, at a school for the deaf.

I take my eyes off the noticeboard and look ahead, to where I need to go.

Then I catch up with the girls.

chapter 4

The blinds are drawn in the classroom, and it takes a moment
for my eyes to adjust.

It looks like there are just the same kids in English as
from my homeroom. I probably should have guessed that.
At my old school there were twenty-two in my class. I tuck
the information away. It will be a good statistic to take home
to Mum.

The desks are arranged in a semi-circle. I put my books
on the desk closest to the door and sit down. Keisha and
Erica sit next to me

'Is this everyone?' I sign to Erica.

Erica nods. Then she goes around the room, pointing
at people. It's kind of embarrassing that she's making it so
obvious that she's telling me about them, but I can't really
do anything about it.

'That's A-d-a-m,' she signs, pointing at a guy with hair that
sits out like a ledge. It's short around the sides, doesn't even
cover his geeky pink hearing aids.

'That's L-i-n-g,' Erica continues, pointing to the girl next
to Adam.

Ling is wearing glasses, but I can still see that one eye goes towards Adam and the other wanders in another direction. It makes her a bit weird-looking.

Erica continues pointing and signing the names of the other kids. The rest look pretty normal.

'So we're all here except for S-t-e-l-l-a,' finishes Erica. 'She's …'

There's something about a plane in there, so I gather that Stella must be away. I don't catch where. Somewhere that begins with an 'A', I think, but Erica's finger spelling is too fast for me. I don't want to ask her to tell me all over again.

So I nod. Pretend I got it. And I try not to let my frustration take over. I'm pretty good at squashing down my feelings now, pretty good at controlling the panic inside me. I even manage a smile at Erica.

The classroom light flicks on and off, on and off. I look up, expecting to see one of the boys mucking around with the light switch. Instead I see a man, clearly a teacher.

'Hi, everyone,' he signs as he walks into the centre of the room. Then he looks directly at me so that everyone else looks at me too. 'Welcome to our class, D-e-m-i. My name is A-l-i-s-t-a-i-r.'

I nod and hope he'll look away. But he doesn't. He gives me a big smile that is obviously supposed to be welcoming but is just making me uncomfortable.

'I started at the College for the Deaf last year, so I'm pretty new too.' His signing is really slow, slower than mine, so I'm getting everything.

'Four years ago I was lucky enough to go to a performance by Theatre of the Deaf,' he continues.

I wish he would stop looking at me. I don't really care whether he went to a performance by Theatre of the Deaf.

It's a relief when he looks away from me and around the classroom, as though that little intro was just for me, but now he's ready to make a larger point to the whole class.

'I fell in love with sign. It's so beautiful. So expressive. I decided I wanted to change my life, to combine my love of sign with my love of teaching.'

I don't feel relieved anymore. I'm irritated. He's clearly not deaf. All that stuff about how beautiful sign language is. Maybe it is beautiful if you have a choice about it. If you haven't been shoved into a silent, hopeless world you know nothing about and don't want to be in. I imagine for a moment what it would be like to have a normal life, to have my hearing, and then to come to this school to *help*.

I don't want to be his project. I close my eyes and block Alistair out.

Jules believes in wishes. Jules says it's to do with putting good energy out into the universe to get it back. I'd love to believe that it works. For the millionth time I tell myself that if the universe restores my hearing, I will do something good and noble like work with the poor in Bangladesh.

I try to send out that thought, but then I wonder if that's exactly what Alistair is doing. I guess the poor people of Bangladesh might think I'm making them my project.

I've probably ruined my wish by thinking that.

I open my eyes. I still can't hear. And Alistair is still signing.

I glance at Keisha. She smiles at me and rolls her eyes. Under the table, she points to herself and signs no. Then she points at Alistair and signs yes, and then the word chatter lots of times in a row. It's like blah blah blah. I get that she's saying that Alistair is the one who goes on and on and deserves the deaf name Chatter more than she does.

And I get that she's endured these speeches from Alistair before. It makes me feel better. Like she has the same response to Alistair and his *help*.

'Sign is expressive and emotional,' Alistair goes on, completely clueless, 'like the poems of K-e-a-t-s. We'll be studying Keats this term.'

He looks around as though he's expecting a round of applause.

I see two looks passing over Alistair's face in quick succession. Before I went deaf I probably wouldn't have even noticed. Jules spent ages teaching me how to read faces, to understand body language.

The first look is disappointment that his speech hasn't got a reaction. That's in the droop of his shoulders, the slight downturn of his mouth.

Then there's a fresh determination. His mouth straightens up and his shoulders push back.

Alistair is so here to *make a difference.* It's almost funny.

He hands out a poem, *A Thing of Beauty*, and asks for a volunteer to come out and sign the poem for the class. I look at the floor.

Finally, Ling gets up. She has a wonky eye and she's deaf and she's up the front signing a poem about beauty. It's kind of embarrassing, and I wonder what my old group of friends would have thought. Stavros can do something similar to Ling with his eyes. It's part of his weird-talents repertoire though, not a permanent condition. Like Shae can jut out her shoulder bones to make shark fins and Nadia can wiggle her ears.

I can imagine them, trying not to laugh, but at the same time egging each other on. I imagine me doing the same, joining in. Not to be cruel, but *come on*. It's funny, right?

I have to remind myself that things are different now. I wouldn't laugh like that anymore, but I know that others will laugh at me.

I remind myself I'm here to learn. I have to get good marks. I'm not even sure if it's still possible to do what I want to do, to be what I want to be, now I'm deaf. But I have to try.

So I kick the gang out of my head. It's not that difficult to do. It's not like I've felt that close to them lately.

chapter 5

The tram takes me right to the street of my favourite pool. There's an electric feeling in the air. I sense it before I see the lightning. Out of habit I count down to the thunder I will never hear. One cat-and-dog, two cat-and-dog, three cat-and-dog. I'm up to seven when I think it must have come, because some kids outside the pool gate are acting afraid, screaming silent screams and hugging each other.

I miss thunder. I used to love storms. Now they're just another reminder that I'm living with the world on mute.

Sometimes I imagine I have a remote control, and if I could only find the right button to press, I'd be able to fix things.

I'd be able to fix me.

It's easier to get to the pool from the deaf school than from my old school. I'm glad I put my swimming stuff in my bag this morning.

Swimming is the one thing that hasn't really changed. It's the one thing that's nearly the same as before.

Even before I get in the water, there's a feeling of comfort. I don't stand out. I'm just there to do laps. Just another anonymous swimmer.

The woman behind the front desk has been there forever. She was there way before I went deaf. I don't think she even knows. She's skinny and wrinkly and her hair is the sort of greeny colour that blondes go when they spend too much time in chlorine.

The lines on her face are like a map of misery. She only ever says one thing, so I don't even really need to lip-read; don't have to concentrate.

'You a member?'

All I have to do is nod and hand her my card.

I walk down the concrete corridor, breathing the familiar smell of dampness and chlorine.

There is a special changing room for the disabled, with a wheelchair sticker peeling off the door. I used to change there, before, if the regular change rooms were busy. I liked the extra space.

Now I keep to the opposite side of the corridor, giving that room a wide berth. As though it could reach out and suck me in if I got too close.

The normal changing room is empty. I quickly change into my bathers. I tie my hair in a ponytail and then tuck it into my bathing cap. It's always a struggle to get all my hair in.

The mirror gives me a misty view of a normal girl in bathers and swimming cap.

I walk out to the pool. The lap lanes are pretty full. I don't feel like fighting for territory today. I sneak a glance at the front desk. The woman is reading a magazine, not paying attention. I decide to risk doing my laps in the empty aqua-play area, roped off from the lap lanes.

I adjust my goggles and dive in. After the first two laps, the tempo kicks in. The tension in my shoulders is gone. One, two, three, breathe.

There are ripples coming from the closest lane, reminding me there are others using the pool. They are deaf too. Everyone is deaf underwater. I am no different.

I used to struggle with the silence when I swam. I used to wish that the pool had music underwater, like some pools do. It seemed boring, just having the thoughts in my head. But I don't feel that way anymore. Maybe I'm finally getting used to the silence.

I think back over my day. I think of Helena stomping and Erica's cochlear sticking out for everyone to see. I think of Alistair and his romantic notions about deafness. It all seems surreal, like the memories of another girl's day.

I miss my old friends. And not just because they were normal. Are normal. Even if the kids at my new school weren't deaf, they still couldn't replace my old friends.

I turn at the end of the pool. When I push out, I find myself thinking about that last sleepover at Nadia's.

It was a Saturday. We were all watching a DVD – with subtitles for me. Well, half-watching a DVD. Stavros and Lockie were revved up, and Lockie kept moving in front of the TV to break dance. He wasn't very good.

Nadia was acting pissed off. I could see that she was yelling at him to move, but it egged him on like a red rag to a bull. I was still sort of trying to follow the movie, but I didn't really care. I was distracted, and not only by Lockie and his terrible moves. Shae kept sneaking looks at Stavros. I'd never noticed her doing it before, and I wondered if it was a new crush or if it had always been there and I was only seeing it now I studied people's faces and body language so closely.

The lounge door opened and Nadia's dad was there. He seemed to be complaining about the noise. We probably were being noisy but of course I didn't really know. Nadia's little brother Jasper appeared beside his dad.

'What's going on?' he asked.

'Show them, Lockie,' I said, and I didn't worry about whether I sounded weird, because these were my friends.

Lockie didn't need much encouragement. Jasper watched him, appalled. He moved to the centre of the room, blocking the TV and taking Lockie's place.

Nadia rolled her eyes with embarrassment, but I was impressed. Jasper was light on his feet and his arms easily supported him when he flipped into a handstand. Lockie moved beside him, mirroring Jasper's cool moves with his own clunky ones. Everyone cracked up.

I loved it. I remember thinking that I might be deaf but that I still belonged there with my friends.

I push off the wall into another lap. My rhythm is being altered by the waves from the action in the lane next to me. I move back to the left-hand side of the lane. I focus on my stroke for a lap, still thinking of that moment at Nadia's.

I slowly realise I am in perfect sync with the swimmer in the lane next to me. Every time I lift my head to breathe on that side, I see him lifting his. Our arms rise up together, slice the water together. It works that way for a whole lap. We touch the wall at the same time. When I turn, though, he's switched to butterfly and the moment is gone.

I switch to breaststroke. I don't have the best technique, but I go deep, right down with the stroke. I could do breaststroke forever. It's like moving between two worlds. The underwater one is blue and dense and the black line at the bottom of the pool stays put. The world above is lighter, and the black line beneath the surface splays and shifts like a trick.

I do a couple of laps, enjoying the easy transition between

the air and the water. Up ahead there's a group of guys gathered around the edge of the pool. Their coach looks serious. He has swimmer's arms, a drinker's belly and skinny legs. He reminds me of a flip book I had when I was young, where you match a giraffe's head to a monkey's torso to a pelican's legs. The coach gets the guys lined up, and they start diving in, one by one.

The guy next in line to dive looks at me. He's cute. I think he's smiling but I might be wrong. For some reason I feel sure he was the one who was swimming in sync with me.

I go under. I'm at the end of the pool, about to do another flip, when I feel a hand placed firmly on my head. It's the skinny blonde from reception. Her mouth is moving and her eyes are narrowed, angry.

She's talking quickly and I don't get it but I know it's because I'm swimming in the wrong section. She looks mad, like she's been yelling. She thinks I've been ignoring her. I feel my face flushing with anger and embarrassment.

I hate this sort of thing. It's moments like this when I think I might actually like it if everyone could tell that I'm deaf. Would it be better if they knew instantly, like with Erica and her cochlear implant? Or others that wear hearing aids? Of course, it wouldn't help once I was in the pool – I'd have to take them off anyway.

I stand up. I duck under the lane rope to the lap lane

and swim off, wanting the cool water to wash away the humiliation. The now-familiar feeling of missing out on the details, of being on the outer, makes me think again of that day at Nadia's.

After the boys went home, Nadia, Shae and I lined up our mattresses, three in a row. Shae was in the middle and I was wishing that I was, and wondering if I could say anything.

Nadia got up, pulling her bunny dressing gown around her. It was the one with little rabbits hopping in different directions. It's really daggy. It's my favourite.

I couldn't believe it when Nadia turned the light off without telling me.

I wanted us all to go to sleep, because I was blocked out now. Out of any conversation. But I could just see their lips moving in the dark, so I knew they were still talking. They were both on their backs, talking up at the ceiling. They were probably whispering their night secrets but how would I know?

It felt horribly familiar. Even at school, in broad daylight, half the time I felt like everyone was whispering secrets. Every time I couldn't make out what someone was saying by lip-reading, every time someone turned away, or covered their mouths so I couldn't follow what was being said, I wondered what I was missing out on.

I don't know if Nadia and Shae had just forgotten that

I couldn't hear them, or if they didn't care. Either way my friends were ignoring me. I didn't know what they were saying. And they were obviously saying *a lot*. Shae might even have been sharing her feelings about Stavros.

Cold fear rushed through me. Maybe they weren't ignoring me. Maybe they were whispering *about* me.

I propped my head up to get a better look at them. Their mouths were moving at the same time, making the same shapes. They were singing.

Somehow it was just as bad as being whispered about. I didn't even know what the song was.

I switch back from breaststroke to freestyle mid-lap. I am eager to move away from the memory now.

From that night, I ditched the sleepovers. I gave myself a curfew, made excuses. But I didn't know that what was coming would come anyway.

I swim faster, but it doesn't help. Now that I've started, a whole tangle of things I don't want to think about are flashing through my mind.

The fight with Nadia on the oval that day.

Making a fool of myself with Jules.

I keep breathing, keep swimming, but my mind is on fast forward and, as if the fight and the stuff with Jules isn't enough, I start thinking about that day at Northfield. The thing I *really* don't want to remember.

I think of that huge guard, his hand heavy on my shoulder. I think of the panic overwhelming me, and the feeling of not getting enough oxygen. But mostly I think of all those people looking at me with disgust – or was it pity?

I've had enough for today. I swim to the side of the pool where the steps are and get out.

chapter 6

Flawless has a new green Saab. It gleams in our driveway, making Dad's ute look extra dirty. I bite my lip as I edge past it. I'm glad that the boys will be here, but with Flawless and Mum around, the interrogation will be planned and there'll be no escape.

I put down my school bag. I need a minute to prepare for their onslaught.

I can see them through the kitchen window. They make a great team. Flawless always agrees with Mum, and Mum loves to be agreed with. I am the perfect subject for them, and the way Flawless is nodding as she chops vegetables makes me think that I'm being discussed right now.

Flawless was twelve when I was born. She wasn't Flawless to me back then. She was Felicity, and I adored her. I was heartbroken whenever she went to stay with her own mum, and was always rapt when she came home. I loved it when people said we both looked like Dad. That she was a fair version, and I was the dark one. I copied the way she dressed and the way she spoke. I followed her around everywhere.

I was only eight when she met Ryan. They were both at uni, both studying law. Ryan was a few years older. He already had his own house and car. I could see why my sister fell for him. He was a handsome mature-age student. Except that he wasn't very mature – he was really funny. He would put a pillow up the back of his T-shirt and pretend to be the hunchback of Notre Dame. He used to lope around chasing me until I squealed for Felicity to come and rescue me.

Felicity didn't finish her law degree. She got pregnant and had Harry instead.

I loved being a nine-year-old auntie. And back then Felicity was still fun. Ryan was pretty successful by the time they had Oscar. But it was like the richer they got, the more boring Felicity became. She stopped being funny and got all serious, all mature and sensible and perfect. It was in high school that Nadia and I started secretly calling her Flawless, and it was so right it just stuck.

These days it's like all she cares about, other than the boys, is her perfect house and going to the gym and getting her hair done and agreeing with Mum.

I pick up my bag again. It feels heavier than before. I let myself in and head to the lounge room.

Harry and Oscar have used their unsupervised playtime excellently. Their faces are both covered in black texta.

Harry is just about to add some more art to Oscar's nose when he sees me.

'Hello,' he signs, lifting his hand and my spirits. His smile is missing two front teeth.

Oscar lies back on the carpet like an upturned bug. It's my signal to tickle. So I kneel next to him and go for it. I wish I could hear him laugh. He's three now. He was only one when I went deaf. His laugh has probably changed. But I do see how his eyes squint as his chubby cheeks take over his face.

His little legs are cycling in the air, and I turn to avoid getting a knee in the face. Felicity is standing in the doorway. I don't know how long she's been there. She is wearing a pink Ralph Lauren polo, collar upturned, and perfectly white jeans.

'Harry! Oscar! Bathroom!' She wouldn't be yelling; that would look like she'd lost control. But she quickly gets hold of Harry's hand and then pulls Oscar out of his dead-bug position, ready for the drag to the bathroom.

'Hi, Demi,' she says, as the boys squirm on either side of her. 'I can't wait to hear about your day.'

I lean against the couch. Flawless exits and Mum enters. They should have a baton.

'Long day?' Mum asks in sign, and the fact that she doesn't say it too, like she would normally, is a warning to me.

It's designed to remind me that she is pretty good at sign language – that we have already made adjustments in our house to cope with my deafness. So this new adjustment, this new school, is unnecessary.

She's wearing her concerned look. It says, 'don't worry, we will be here for you when you change your mind and make the *right* decision' more clearly than any sign could.

'No, it wasn't a long day. It was good,' I say. I don't sign it at all.

If there's a kind of scoring system going on with her signing and me voicing then I think we're about even.

'Great,' Mum signs. 'Tell us at dinner.'

It feels like a threat.

Felicity sits with a straight back. Her gym-toned arm reaches for the salt and moves it out of Harry's reach. Mum nods her approval.

'Jim?' Mum says, frowning.

Dad is eating with his left hand and writing in his notepad with his right.

'Where's Ryan?' I ask with my voice.

Dad sneaks me a wink. He and I do this for each other. We change the subject if Mum's about to go into nag mode.

Felicity places her hands on the table. Her fingers are splayed, showing off the white tips of her French manicure like they're some kind of achievement.

I fold my hands, hiding my short, bitten nails under the table.

'Ryan's working on a …' Felicity turns sideways towards Mum so I don't catch the rest of the sentence. She does that quite often, even though she says she understands how important it is not to. I can generally fill in the gaps though. Most likely, he's working on a case.

'So Demi, how was it?' Felicity asks, turning to face me again. Even though it's easy to lip-read her now, she adds some signing for effect.

'Yes Demi, how was it?' Mum says, like an echo.

Mum reverts to her concerned look. I suspect she's hoping it didn't go so well and that I'll have changed my mind.

'It was good,' I say with my voice.

I don't worry too much about how I sound. Not with my family. But even after all this time it still feels like I've got headphones on, and I have to trust that the vibrations in my throat will guide me to keep my voice somewhere between a whisper and a scream.

'The class sizes are really small. There are only eight kids in my class. Well, nine actually, but one girl wasn't there. And you know how I used to miss stuff when Jules wasn't there to interpret for me? Well, the notes from every class are put up on the school intranet.'

I'm convincing myself as I go. I am trying to modulate my voice with ups and downs to convince them at the same time. If I'm not careful, Mum will sniff out the doubt. I'm about to tell her about the fortnightly elective speech therapy sessions when Mum makes the sign for me to lower my volume. Two hands pushing downwards.

I hate that sign. I really do. It means that I'm not getting it right. Again. Like I got it wrong at speech night. The thought makes me shudder, makes me cast my eyes downwards.

Mum reaches over, gently tapping the table in front of me to get my attention.

'Do you sign or voice in your English class?' she asks with her mouth, and she looks a bit impatient, like she might be asking for a second time.

'We mostly signed today, but the teacher's hearing so he can obviously speak,' I reply. 'I think we'll do a bit of both. And my homeroom teacher does both too.'

'… not right', Mum is saying, and I get straight away that she's choosing to focus on the signing in today's class and nothing else. It's annoying that she hasn't even acknowledged the small class sizes. 'It's really important … speak so you can operate … hearing world, don't you think?'

Normally I get pretty much everything Mum says, but

she's now addressing everyone at the table, so her head is swivelling, challenging each of us in turn. As she finishes, she looks straight at me, but she doesn't mean it as a question, so I don't bother to answer. I don't remind her that most English assessments are written anyway, or that the students are all deaf, so *of course* the teacher needs to sign.

She just makes me more determined to pick out the bits from my day that I want to tell. If Mum can flick away the information she wants to flick away, then so can I.

I breathe. I don't feel like talking anymore, and I can see Mum getting fidgety, patting her left hand with her right as though she's counting how long I'm being silent. It stresses Mum out to think that I might forget how to speak. It totally freaked her out when I stopped talking for a whole week. When I wouldn't go to school, wouldn't leave the house, didn't want to see *anyone.*

After Northfield. That horrible day.

I wouldn't tell Mum what happened. Couldn't tell anyone. But even though I couldn't share it, I played what had happened over and over in my mind, as though going over it might let me change it somehow. Or at least wear out the memory so it no longer bothered me.

The thing is, Mum wasn't the only one freaking out. I freaked myself out, too. I'm pretty sure that week took its toll on my speech, though of course it's impossible for me to tell. I wanted to be able to keep speaking. But I just shut down after Northfield.

Dad's hand pats the table in front of me. It's a save. Well, an attempted save.

'... it interesting?' he says with a wink.

Dad's trimmed his handlebar moustache so I can see his mouth better, but I still find myself watching the hair on his upper lip bounce up and down, not catching very much of what he's saying. I told him the trim worked fine because I knew he didn't want to shave it all off, and anyway, it's kind of comforting. I don't want him to change. I want him to stay the way he's always been.

'... other classes – '

I can tell Mum has cut him off by the way he's stopped talking. His eyes swerve towards her and she's off again.

'I spoke to Jules today,' she says, her attention fully aimed towards me now. 'He thinks there's a chance we could get more funding. It's possible he could be there full time instead of three days. If we ever wanted to go back to your old school.'

It's unbelievable. She still thinks that getting a sign teacher and interpreter to be with me full time, rather than just three days, might convince me to go back to my *normal* school. She's been playing around with this idea for ages but there's never been enough funding. A while ago I would have agreed that it would make all the difference. I would have loved having Jules there every day.

But it wouldn't help now. It's too late, too much has happened. And I am not sure I even want it anymore. I always dread seeing Jules now, after what I did.

'Mum,' I say firmly, '*we* understood everything the teachers said today. Not like at my old school.'

I've tried to put a sarcastic slant on the 'we'. But I can't be sure of that sort of effect anymore, and it still shits me. I was the queen of sarcasm before I went deaf.

'I understood what everyone was on about.' I say it straight this time.

Mum nods. Her face has relaxed a bit, now I've spoken again. She pauses, as if she's gathering her thoughts. But we all know her well enough to know that they're already gathered. She's just figuring out her delivery.

'That's great, Demi,' she says. 'It's just an option.'

Flawless is sitting next to Mum. Her mouth is moving, but her eyes are on Harry. He's pushing peas under a mound of mashed potatoes. It's pretty funny, but of course Felicity is not amused. She leans across to him and pulls them out with her fork, one by one. I presume she's giving Harry a lecture. When he glances at me, I give him a wink like the one Dad gave me.

I feel Felicity's eyes on me. I look at her properly for the first time that night. She looks as perfect as ever, but still I notice there's something different. She looks tired, her eyes somehow duller.

'See? Mum's right,' she's saying. I realise that she's at the end of her little speech, and that it was aimed at me and not at Harry and his pea mutiny. '... nice to have options like Jules.'

I zone out. Felicity has swallowed Mum's philosophies as a pre-dinner snack. It's quite a skill that she is able to regurgitate them whole.

'Anyway, just a thought,' Mum says with a shrug suggesting it's all very casual.

It's a thought that surrounds me. A thought that seeps into every nook and cranny of my life.

chapter 7

After dinner, Mum puts the boys to bed while Flawless does the dishes. Mum goes back into the kitchen. I can see them through the doorway, sitting next to each other on barstools at the kitchen bench. The two of them chat away like girlfriends.

I go into the lounge room. I choose one end of the couch, and Dad chooses the other. I put my feet on his lap and we watch *Law and Order, S.V.U.*

I always hated subtitles. Now I'm stuck with them for any TV show – I rely on them. It's funny, but I hate subtitles even more than I used to. I can tell they're not accurate, that they only give the viewer a small taste of the detail.

Rock music plays inside, explain the subtitles. But what does that mean? Is it modern rock or old rock? It makes a difference. *Dog barks.* Is it the bark of a big, mean dog or the yap of a cute little poodle?

It's just like my life. I'm always trying to figure out what's really going on. Always having to fill in the gaps, but never getting all the details. It's like trying to do a jigsaw when I don't even know what the picture is, and I'm missing one of the vital middle pieces.

Now, I get that Rin is speaking, though he's off camera. His name comes up in a box, and his dialogue is beside it. I know he's a man of few words, so I probably don't miss much. But when Olivia goes off on one of her major rants, and the same words stay on the screen for ages, I know I'm missing out on a stack of detail and it drives me crazy.

It's just like the day I had the fight with Nadia. When everything I'd been bottling up erupted.

Dad is writing stuff down. He's taking notes on what the subtitles have missed, and hands me them in the ads.

It's a gift, though I know he doesn't think that way. He just does it.

I snuggle down again. My feet touch Dad's. He's wearing his old woolly Explorer socks.

S.V.U comes back on. The case has gone to trial. The district attorney is smart. I love how she lines up her closing argument and trips the crim over his own lies. She's exactly who you'd want to be, if you could choose.

Dad writes as he watches. He knows this is my favourite part of the show, so he's more thorough now. He flags the last few words that have been subtitled and then jots down the words they've missed or misrepresented.

There's another ad break, and I have time to read Dad's notes. When the show comes on again, it's only a wrap up.

The notebook is resting on Dad's chest, suggesting that he doesn't feel the need to catch me up. That I've got the whole plot.

For once.

I'm in bed and still reading when Mum comes to the door.

'Night, Demi,' she says. I put my book face down beside me.

'Why are the boys sleeping here again?' I ask.

I see Mum sucking in a breath, pausing before she answers.

'She has a ... morning,' Mum says. She's not quite looking at me, so I don't catch everything.

'A what morning?' I ask.

This time, Mum signs what I've missed. An appointment. I've had enough appointments in the last few years to know the sign perfectly.

I roll my eyes. Mum seems to be looking after the boys a lot lately. I wonder what Felicity's appointment is. She's probably broken a nail or needs a wax. *Emergency!*

'Night,' I say, picking up my book again.

There's a strange look on Mum's face. I can't read it. Maybe she's just tired.

'I want *you* to be happy,' she signs, and the way she points to me while she's signing is a bit confusing.

Does she mean, simply, that she wants me to be happy? Or does she mean she wants me to be happier than someone else? I'm not sure, but Mum is already moving on.

'Did something happen with Jules?' she asks with her voice now. 'You still like him, don't you?'

'Yeah, of course,' I say, faking a yawn.

She leans against the doorframe. She is frowning, like she doesn't entirely believe me.

I look down at the page so I don't have to make eye contact. And then I look back at Mum, because she's still standing there.

'Just think about what I said,' she says, as she slowly turns to leave.

I try to go back to my book, but Mum's suggestion has taken. I think about Jules.

I met him during the rodeo ride of specialists. We were still hopeful I'd get my hearing back. But we were hedging our bets. I was learning sign, just in case my condition was permanent.

We were still being given casseroles, lasagnas and sympathy. But Jules didn't walk into my life with sympathy. He walked in with intent. He told me how his sister had been deaf from birth, and that it never stopped her from doing anything he did.

And he taught me to sign.

Jules and I sat together on stools in the bathroom for many of our early lessons. I watched his mouth in the mirror practising lip-reading and signing. Sometimes there was a bit of stubble on his upper lip. Sometimes there was smoothness. There was always a smile in his eyes.

When I went back to school, he was there with me three days a week. He would stand beside the teacher, making sure I understood. I can still see him now, if I try. I can see Jules standing next to Dr Tolley, my chem teacher. He is wearing white volleys, jeans and a yellow Che Guevara T-shirt. He is signing instructions for an experiment. Dr Tolley has a well-earned reputation for being long winded. He goes on and on, but I'm saved from the droning. He keeps looking over at Jules, as though he can check that he's being interpreted correctly, though of course he has no idea about signing.

It's funny, because Jules's signing takes a fraction of Tolley's droning time. My friends get the joke. There are lots of smiles in my direction. I feel good.

The other kids liked him. There was nothing not to like. He was young and cool.

And he was mine.

At least, that's what I started to think. Stupid girl. Stupid deaf girl.

chapter 8

'L-u-k-e thinks you're hot.' Keisha is signing to me under her jumper. I'm the only one who can see her signing, so I guess she's telling me a secret. I'm not fussed about Luke gossip, but it's nice to have someone telling me something private, after all this time of feeling like I am missing out on secrets.

We are out in the school garden, doing hands-on plant identification for biology.

'He thinks green eyes and brown hair are the best,' she continues.

I look closely at Keisha. Her eyes are so puppy dog sad that she looks like a cartoon version of herself. Even without Erica's comment yesterday, it's not hard to figure out that she likes Luke.

'You are hot,' she signs, before she pulls her hands out of her jumper.

I am so not interested. In Luke, or in anyone. Not since Jules.

'Tell him I'm gay,' I sign to Keisha, making an 'O' with my

middle finger and thumb under my own jumper.

'Are you?' Keisha asks, her hands out in the open now. Her eyebrows are raised as she bites her bottom lip. I can tell she's hoping I'm serious.

'No,' I say with a shake of my head, and Keisha laughs. It's an unguarded laugh. Even though I can't hear it, I can tell by the wide smile and the way she throws back her head.

I try not to laugh out loud anymore, because it's harder to control the volume of a laugh and I don't want to sound goofy and deaf. But I do smile at her. She's nice, Keisha or Chatter or whatever I should call her. And she's actually quite normal-looking too, when she's not doing some over-the-top laugh or face. She is about the same height and build as me. She has shoulder-length chocolatey hair that's dead straight so that the layers work properly. Mine will only be straight until lunchtime, when my morning hair-straightening session always loses out to nature.

'Sorry to interrupt,' our teacher Morris signs right in front of our faces. 'Can you repeat what I said about this tree? What is it?'

'B-a-n-k-s-i-a,' Keisha signs. I didn't know that.

'Yes!' Morris is clearly excited that Keisha knew the answer. 'What kingdom?' he asks.

There are four people in our biology class. Keisha, Erica, Cam – the blond guy who sits next to Luke, and me.

We all gather around the tree. Keisha shakes her head and Morris repeats the question, but this time he opens it up to the group. When he scratches his head, I swear I can see dandruff flakes flying into the garden.

'C-a-m?' Morris asks, finger spelling the three letters.

Now Cam is beside me, I can see the combo of his cochlear implant and hearing aids. It's weird, but I don't think they look so bad today. Maybe they're only really ugly if you zoom in on them. Or maybe I'm just getting used to them.

'Plantae,' Cam says.

Even though I can't hear him, I can see from the shape his mouth makes that he has mispronounced the word. He said plantee. I wonder if Morris will correct him. I wonder if it matters, here.

'-ay,' Morris says, making the distinctive shape with his mouth, giving me my answer. 'Plant-ae.'

I'm glad. I want to be corrected if I make a mistake. I want to be pushed to pronounce things properly, and I want people to tell me if I'm speaking too loudly or too quietly. Even when it makes me feel like a fool.

Mum would approve of Morris correcting Cam. I tuck the info away. I'm sure I'll be pulling it out sometime soon.

Cam repeats the word, correctly this time. He glances at me, Keisha and Erica and grins. When Morris turns away, Cam scratches his own head and mimes a whole load of stuff flying out. Then, he mimes a plant growing extra-quick, as though the dandruff is a magic fertiliser.

When Morris turns back, Cam's hands freeze midway through some serious plant growth. It's pretty funny.

Morris taps his watch, then points up to the roof of the school building. The red light is flashing. I'm surprised it's lunchtime already.

'Meet you back here with food?' Cam asks us, and it seems I'm being included without a thought. And even though they're just a bunch of deaf students, it feels nice.

Luke is with Cam when they join us for lunch. I am sitting on one side of the bench, and Erica and Keisha are on the other. When Luke sits right next to me, I move up a bit. So does he. I feel squirmy.

'You are beautiful,' he signs, a muesli bar taking the place of a finger. Now I feel squirmier. 'I love you!'

I get a flush of embarrassment, as much for Luke as for me. He's too old to be acting like this, and I'm too old to have to handle it. It's so *obvious*. So immature. It's like he's not just deaf, but also simple or something. I can hardly believe that he's still staring at me, waiting for a reaction.

'I'm not available,' I sign, feeling ridiculous. Especially

since the sign for 'available' should have my right hand doing a rotation clockwise. I've gone anticlockwise. The others are all grinning, but I can tell it's only Keisha who's paying any real attention.

'You're breaking my heart!' Luke signs, pumping his hands over his heart and throwing his head back, and I feel a sense of relief now that he's being deliberately over the top. It's some kind of show, or maybe just a joke. 'You've got to love me. Check out my eyelashes!' He splays the fingers of both hands above his eyes dramatically.

'It's best to ignore him.' Erica interrupts Luke's signing of eyelashes by waving her own hands over the top of them. 'He falls in love all the time. He'll get over it.'

Keisha is frowning. She grabs Erica's hand, and pulls her away from the table. The two of them walk to the far end of the garden. It feels awkward, being left here with just the boys. When they start up a conversation about footy, I try to act interested, but I'm not. They're going too fast for me anyway.

I can't help looking down to the end of the garden at Keisha and Erica. Keisha has her back to me, so I can't see what she's saying. Maybe she'll hate me because Luke likes me when she so obviously likes him. Maybe she's talking to Erica about me right now. Will Erica go off me too, if Keisha does? The thing is, I don't know for sure what they're talking about. But I know I'm missing out. Again.

It makes me think of that day I lost it with Nadia.

It was lunchtime, and Nadia and Shae were on the other side of the oval. I could see Nadia rubbing Shae's back, and I could tell that Shae was sobbing. Her shoulders rose up and down with the sobs.

I was worried. Shae was tough. She hardly ever cried, so whatever had happened must have been pretty full-on. I started to walk across the oval to them.

I was about halfway there when a football slammed into my back. It hurt. I turned to see two year seven boys running towards me. They were too far away for me to lip-read everything, but they were clearly saying sorry.

'I'm OK,' I said, through clenched teeth when they got closer. I wasn't OK. I was sure there would be a bruise on my back by morning. But I gritted my teeth and kept walking.

'What? What is it?' I asked Nadia when I got closer. My back was throbbing as I squatted down beside my friends.

Shae said something to Nadia that I couldn't see.

'It's OK, Demi,' Nadia said. 'Shae's OK. Don't worry about it.'

I'm good at lip-reading that phrase. I get it all the time. When I ask people to repeat what they said, something I've missed, I often get that phrase. When I miss the punch line to a joke that others have since decided wasn't very funny, I get that phrase.

But I want to decide what's funny or important or worth worrying about for myself.

'Just tell me what happened!' I said. I was frustrated, and probably speaking too loudly.

'Jesus, Demi,' Nadia said, and she rolled her eyes and shook her head like I was just being annoying.

Nadia's hand was still on Shae's back. It hurt, looking at it – a reminder that she was able to comfort Shae because she knew what was wrong.

'You ... it's always about you all the time,' continued Nadia. She looked angry, and I could tell she was speaking loudly, maybe even yelling, by the way her face was moving and her mouth was forming the words. '... went deaf. But it's not all about you, OK?'

I felt sick. I felt shaky with the sickness of not knowing anything, of not being told and of not understanding. I felt sick because of my throbbing back and my aching heart and my useless ears. I was sick of people glaring at me because they'd said hello and I hadn't answered. Or because they'd asked me a question then looked at me like I was the rudest person alive when I didn't reply.

It was *not* always about me! It was hardly *ever* about me, because *nobody* really understood!

'You are a massive bitch,' I said, and spat out the words like I had no control over what I was saying.

Nadia and Shae looked shocked. They looked shocked *together*, just like they sang *together* when the lights were switched off and I didn't even know what the song was.

They looked at each other like I was some kind of freak. Then Nadia stood up, her hands on her hips as she glared at me.

I took off then, angrily brushing away the tears. I ran back across the oval, away from my so-called friends.

Luke's hand moves in front of my face.

'Are you daydreaming about me?' He mouths it as well as signing.

'Sorry,' I sign. 'You're going too fast for me. It's better when you sign and speak together. That way I can lip-read as well.'

'Don't get too used to it,' Erica signs as she and Keisha sit back down on the bench. Keisha responds to my 'I hope we're OK' smile with a big, full one. She seems fine, as though her chat with Erica has helped. Anyway, she doesn't seem to be holding any grudges against me. 'S-t-e-l-l-a is back next week.'

I'm confused. It must show on my face, because Erica explains.

'When Stella is around, we mostly sign,' she says. 'She doesn't speak or mouth at all.'

'Oh,' I respond, but I don't really understand.

'Her parents are both deaf, so she's never needed to learn to speak,' says Keisha.

'Yeah right,' says Cam. 'As if Star would use her voice even if she could!'

I raise my eyebrows at him, asking wordlessly what he means.

'When Star is around we do things her way. We bow and scrape,' Cam explains. I gather that Star must be Stella's deaf name.

I still don't really know what Cam's on about but it seems that Stella has some serious power around here.

'I can't wait to see her,' Erica says. 'She's very cool,' she says to me.

'Icy even,' Luke adds with a grin. His broken heart seems to have mended.

The teacher on yard duty signs to us that lunchtime is over. When Luke gets up, Keisha hurries over to join him.

I can see what she's signing, even from a distance, because she's half-facing me, walking backwards in front of Luke. It's public, even though she probably doesn't want it to be. All I have to do is look, and I guess that's worth remembering for the future, in case I ever want to say something private.

But I'm glad I can see this. I'm glad I'm not locked out. It's so cute.

'I like your eyelashes,' she signs.

chapter 9

It's Friday afternoon. I've had an OK week. In fact, it's been better than OK. I'm starting to feel settled.

Erica and Keisha are loading books into their bags for weekend homework. I do the same.

'What are you doing now?' Erica asks.

'Why don't you come with us?' Keisha adds.

I heave my laden school bag onto my back so I can sign. 'Come where?' I ask.

'We're going to have a Coke and a look around – '

'I wish I had money,' Erica interrupts. 'I can't buy anything. You're lucky, Chatter.'

'I'm not lucky,' Keisha argues, rolling her eyes. 'I earn my money by working. You know that.'

I wonder what Keisha's job might be. What job could a deaf teenage girl get? But it's hard to get a word, or a sign, in. Finally I manage to ask.

'I work in a cafe,' Keisha signs. 'I love it.'

'How do you do it?' I ask. 'I mean, how do you know you'll get the customer's orders right? Or explain things to them?'

Keisha mimes handwriting. 'It works fine,' she signs.

'Everyone in town knows I'm deaf, so they're used to it.'

I realise I'm staring at Keisha. She's so … I don't know. She's just seems so fine about being deaf. It's as though getting her customers to write down their orders is no big deal. That's just the way it is.

'You're lucky that you're allowed to work,' Erica signs, looking at me like she wants me to agree. 'Mum reckons I've got enough on my plate without working as well. But my clothes are crap and she never buys me new ones.'

I'd like to ask Keisha more about her work, but she's pulling a magazine out of her school bag.

'I want something like this, only cheaper,' Keisha signs.

She shows me a page of celebrities who have been marked out of ten for their outfits. She points to a photo of a blonde, skinny model in a summer dress that probably cost thousands of dollars.

'They only gave her a seven!' she signs, throwing her hands up in disgust. It's funny seeing Keisha get all worked up about the ranking of some celebrity in a magazine.

'This is nice too.' Erica leans over Keisha's shoulder as Keisha points to some model wearing a tiny pink dress. I'm worried Keisha's about to move on to the actress in the next photo, who has scored a measly three for her tie-dyed bikini top, denim short-shorts and stilettos. I agree with the judges on this one. I'm not a fan of the look *or* the girl.

I wave my hand in front of Keisha's face, because I have a feeling this could go on for a long time. 'Where are you going?'

'North f-i-e-l-d', Keisha signs.

There's a wobble inside me and I feel my chest tightening. I can feel the panic growing and spreading, taking hold of me.

Northfield. Northfield.

I have to put my bag down. I have to sit. I make my way to a bench seat at the side of the corridor.

I tell myself I will calm down. I tell myself it's all in my head, which means I can stop it. It's happened before, and I survived those attacks. The first one was after reading Harry's note about my ears. The second one was after the fight with Nadia.

But those attacks were nothing like the one at Northfield. I've never told anyone what happened there.

Keisha and Erica are on another planet. On their planet, there is still enough air for them to continue talking and signing about dresses and models and shopping. I am feeling dizzy, like I've been spinning around and stopped suddenly. Everything's blurred, and I feel like I might throw up.

I can calm down. I can breathe.

'Are you OK?' Erica asks. She and Keisha are standing in front of me. I don't know how they got there, and they still look fuzzy to me. They might have floated over.

'You've gone pale,' Keisha says.

I look down at my hands. They're quivering. I hold on to my thighs to steady them.

I can't talk yet. I can't sign yet. I breathe. Long, deep breaths.

Keisha sits beside me. Her hand is on my back. Erica is crouching in front of me. Her eyes are wide. She is slowly coming back into focus.

'Should we get a teacher?'

I don't think I'm going to vomit. I risk a shake of the head. I free my hands and look at them before I sign. The shaking has settled. I breathe until I feel I can use my hands without the girls noticing.

'I'm fine now. Really.'

Keisha's hand leaves my back. 'You scared me,' she signs. 'Are you asthmatic?'

I nod. I lie. But people who have panic attacks are not quite right. People who have asthma can't help it.

'You look better,' Erica signs. 'Don't you have an asthma puffer?'

I nod and point to my bag. It's another lie. 'But I don't need it.'

I'm getting enough oxygen now, though sometimes my breath comes as a shudder, like it does after a big crying session. I'm exhausted. But it's over.

'Want us to take you home?' Keisha signs. 'We can go shopping another time.'

Erica gives her a look. A 'how about we *don't* take her home and go shopping like we planned?' look. Keisha ignores her.

'No,' I sign. 'But thanks.'

'Then why don't you come with us?' Keisha asks, and as soon as she's finished using her hands to sign she rubs my back again. I wish she wouldn't. It's bad enough that I flipped out in front of them. I just want them to forget what happened. I just want to be left alone.

'I can't come. I've got my nephew's birthday party.'

'Are you an auntie? That's crazy. How old is your nephew?' Erica asks.

'Turning seven,' I answer. 'You want to see a photo?'

I go to my bag to get my phone and also to escape the back rub. I show them the photo of Harry and Oscar that I have as my wallpaper.

'So cute!' Keisha signs.

I can feel myself relaxing a bit. I'm so relieved that the panic attack is over. The girls don't seem to suspect anything and, more importantly, they haven't figured out what started it. A teenager who doesn't want to go shopping is even weirder than a teenager who has panic attacks. I'm secretly relieved

I have Harry's party to go to. Otherwise I would've had to make up some story about not liking big shopping centres or something, and I don't have the energy for that right now.

We all walk together to the tram stop. Keisha and Erica make sure I'm OK before they cross the road to take a tram in the opposite direction.

'Have fun,' I sign to them when they get across the road to their tram stop. Like it wasn't a big deal, what just happened. Like I don't care where they're going. Like it doesn't push any buttons.

'You too,' they sign, as my tram slides between us.

Felicity and Ryan's house is gorgeous. It's large and angular and modern, with lots of windows.

The front door is open, and there are balloons all around the door frame. Mum walks in first, carrying a birthday cake with musical candles. The candles make a robotic, toneless kind of music – I remember that.

Dad trudges in behind Mum. He hates crowds, and we all know there will be one. Flawless wouldn't consider it a proper party otherwise. He turns to look at me.

I cross my eyes and poke out my tongue. He does the same.

There's no-one in the house. We pass into the kitchen so Mum can put down the cake. There are bowls of pita crisps and platters of dip on the bench. On the kitchen table is a neat pile of presents, most of them beautifully wrapped. I know that after the party, Flawless will supervise the unwrapping. She will write down what was from who and get Harry to write thank-you notes within a week.

'Hi, guys,' Flawless says, coming in through the back door. She looks amazing, kind of like a weather girl on TV. She's wearing a bright blue dress that crosses over her chest, and high heels studded with sparkly pink flowers. Her nails and lips are the same shade of pink.

'Oh, how sweet, Dem,' she says, looking at the present in my hands. 'Do you want to put it with the other gifts?'

I finger the present I've brought for Harry. It's wrapped with glossy pages from a magazine, stuck together with masking tape because I couldn't find the regular sticky tape. It's an action figure. I don't want to put it on the table. I want to give it to Harry myself.

Flawless opens the fridge to get something. While her back is turned, I stuff the present into my bag. I'll sneak it to him when I get a chance.

I'm looking down, so I feel the tap-tap of striding heels before I see them.

Felicity's mum. It's always entertaining to see her.

Her hair is platinum blonde, the skin of her face pulled tight. Today she is wearing a red pencil skirt and jacket, and she's towing a man about Ryan's age behind her. The poor guy looks like he's surprised to be here, being led along by this older woman.

Dad always gets a bit fidgety when he sees his ex-wife. I see him shove his hands into his pockets. 'Hello, Vivian,' he greets her.

Vivian air-kisses Dad, completely ignoring my mum. Mum has a funny expression on her face, as though she's eaten something that's gone off, and has nowhere to spit it out.

Vivian gives Felicity a stiff hug. I realise it's a goodbye hug, though the party has only just started.

Felicity watches her mother as she leads her boyfriend down the hall and out the front door. Vivian tosses her head, and her hair shimmers like hair in a shampoo commercial.

We follow Felicity out into the backyard.

It's all happening out there. On the left, there is a marquee with a bar and high tables with stools. Felicity must have hired it all. There seem to be a lot of adults sitting around for a kid's party.

On the other side is a jumping castle with a giant slide. Nearby a pretty woman dressed as a fairy organises a row of children waiting to get their faces painted.

My legs are being hugged. I look down and see that the hugger is a lion.

'Raah,' Harry says, showing me his claws.

'Raah,' I say out loud, hugging him back. 'Happy birthday, Fierce Lion.'

I crouch so that we are face to face.

'Wow,' I say, 'who are all your friends?'

Harry bites a lip, surveying the kids. His face brightens when his eyes land on a little boy who is eating fairy floss and watching other kids come down the slide.

'There he is!' Harry says, turning so I can see his face as he speaks. 'That's A-l-f-i-e.' Harry doesn't know much sign, but he has learnt the alphabet, for me. 'From my class,' he continues.

'Oh,' I say, 'that's great!' But I'm wondering who the other kids are if they're not Harry's friends.

I feel a hand on my shoulder and look up.

'Hi, Dem,' Ryan says, giving me a kiss on the cheek as I stand. His shirt is the same blue as Felicity's dress. She likes things to match.

'How's my favourite sister-in-law?' he signs as he speaks, and even though he gets favourite wrong, holds up the wrong fingers, I like that he's trying.

'You mean your only sister-in-law,' I sign, and he gets it.

He should. We do this all the time.

'Same thing,' he says, completing our ritual.

'I'm good thanks,' I say. 'Started at the new –'

Felicity grabs me by the arm and pulls me over to where she is standing with another woman.

'This is M-a-g-g-i-e S-c-o-t-t. She works with Ryan,' she says, signing at the same time. It takes a while for Felicity to finger spell her name. I guess I should be glad the name isn't longer. Maggie Scott looks at Flawless's fingers, obviously fascinated. 'And over there are her lovely children, L-a-r-a and M-i-a.'

Flawless points. Lara is dressed as a fairy. Her little sister is in the process of having her face painted as a butterfly. Which makes her a caterpillar, I guess, logically.

I feel a flash of anger. These kids aren't even Harry's friends! Felicity has let Harry invite one lousy friend from school. It's all about Felicity having a chance to show off her perfect house and her perfect life to Ryan's work colleagues. She's using her seven-year-old's birthday party to network. It's so selfish!

Maggie seems to be having trouble with her heels. She turns towards me, but one gets stuck in the grass.

'Maggie, this is my little sister, Demi,' Felicity continues.

'OH HELLO!' Maggie says, easing a heel up and out. 'HOW ARE YOU, DEMI? IT'S VERY NICE TO MEET YOU.'

Maggie is speaking loudly. I can tell because there's too

much space between her words. Her mouth is open and round like a laughing clown at a fun park. It's something people sometimes do when they are really uncomfortable taking to someone deaf. It can actually make people harder to understand. I've learnt to lip read when people are speaking normally.

'GOOD THANK YOU,' I say, speaking too loudly and slowly, mimicking her.

I can tell Felicity gets it. Her raised eyebrows are for me, imperceptible to Maggie. Her champagne glass is drained in the next mouthful.

'Maggie is a criminal lawyer,' Felicity says, facing me directly. She turns to Maggie. I can guess what she's saying even if I can't see it properly. Maggie confirms it.

'OH REALLY!' she says to me. 'EVEN THOUGH …?' She stops. Changes direction. 'HOW VERY BRAVE! AND …' She lifts her glass to her lips so the last word is obscured. It might have been ambitious or ridiculous. I only see the 'ous'. I guess the words are pretty much interchangeable anyway.

I wish Felicity hadn't told her.

I wish I could come back at her, say something biting.

I wish I could say that I'm deaf, not *retarded*.

But I've already established what I think of wishes. And anyway, part of me thinks she's right. A big part of me.

It probably is crazy to think I'll get into law. And it's even more mental to think I could handle the courtroom without being able to hear anything that's going on. It wasn't such a crazy dream before I went deaf. But now?

I search for an escape. I look over to the jumping castle and spot Harry. I make my excuses to Maggie and Flawless and head over to him. It's not until I'm close that I see that his painted whiskers are streaked with tears.

'They won't let me go on,' he says, and I can see that Maggie's fairy and butterfly are blocking the entrance to the jumping castle.

I see Harry 'raah' at them, and I get the impression he's been through this routine before. It has no effect on the girls. My heart aches for him. They don't budge.

'Move it,' I say, loudly I think, and the fairy and the butterfly get out of the way.

'Raah,' says Harry one more time. He obviously needs to believe that it was the 'Raah' that moved them on.

I know how he feels.

chapter 10

I sleep in on Saturday. It's afternoon by the time Mum's vacuuming serves its purpose. It used to be her lovely way of encouraging me to get out of bed, but it doesn't work too well anymore. I suppose it's one of the few advantages of being deaf. All I get are the thumps from when she bumps the vacuum cleaner against the wall, and it's not enough to wake me fully.

Anyway, there's no rush to start the day. It's not like I have anything on.

I have breakfast in my pyjamas and go back to my room. I sign in to my email. Nadia's name pops up on MSN. I change my status so I look like I'm offline.

I haven't cleared out my inbox for ages. I know what I'm looking for as I delete emails that tell me how to love and live and laugh and have a better sex life with Viagra. Finally I come to Nadia's email. It was written really late at night, after the wobbly I chucked at school.

To: <u>Demi Valentino (daringdemi@hotmail.com)</u>
From: <u>Nadia Altman (nadiaaltman@yahoo.com)</u>
Sent: Wednesday March 10, 12.54 am
📎 1 attachment/download attachment

Dem. Couldn't sleep. Feel shitty about 2day. Shae was crying about her brother. He found her pin code & stole money out of her account. Loser. She was really upset & kind of embarrassed & it didn't seem like a great time 2 fill u in. Still i feel shit about what happened with u.

I know it's been sooo hard and i didn't mean to yell at u & say that stuff. I know u get left out of things & that sometimes u can't figure out what's going on. So i guess i should have taken the time to let u know what was up?

Anyway if stuff like that ever happens again i promise i'll try harder. I'll take care of u. Ur still my best friend and i hate feeling like this.

Love ya guts

From

Ms (massive) Bitchface (lol)

PS. Open attachments. V cute!

PPS. like argument quote best. Remember how we used to fight heaps??

I vaguely remember opening the attachment when I first got the email. Nadia is always forwarding on some lame thing that you're supposed to send to a hundred of your closest friends for good luck and prosperity and blah blah blah. But I open it again now.

It takes forever to load. There are lots of pictures of dogs hugging cats, that kind of thing. I scroll through them, and then scan the friendship quotes below.

> A simple friend thinks the friendship over when you have an argument. A real friend knows that it's not friendship until you've had a fight – Unknown.

> True friendship is never serene – Marquise de Sevigne.

> Our most difficult task as a friend is to offer understanding when we don't understand – Robert Brault.

The first quote jumps out at me.

Nadia and I used to argue all the time before I went deaf. We argued about who was the coolest guy in school, who was the hottest actor. We argued over who had the bigger lunch, and who in our group could be trusted with a secret. If we got on separate teams in school debates, we went hard. We thrived on arguing.

After I went deaf, we didn't do it anymore. Nadia was always trying to be nice to me, trying to help me. And I kind of lost the urge, anyway. I lost all my fight.

Going deaf and trying to act like I wasn't deaf when

I was struggling just to follow what was going on around me sucked all that extra energy out of me. It sucked my confidence too. I knew I'd probably just sound like a retard if I got too worked up about something.

We might have outgrown the arguing anyway, I guess. Maybe it was just because we were fourteen. But who knows?

We talked about it the next day at school. Nadia said sorry, and so did I. But I left out stuff, because what was the point? Even while we were making up, I kept thinking of the third quote, the one about not understanding.

That quote was ridiculous. It left me cold. How can you understand what you have never been through yourself? How could Nadia ever understand what it was like to be me? She couldn't. Before I went deaf, I would *never* have understood.

Only Jules really understood me. He understood more than anyone else who was hearing what it was like to be deaf, because of his deaf sister. I felt like our signing was a secret language. No-one else in my life signed so well. Sign let us jump into each other's mind so we could really communicate. Jules and I could *relate*. I didn't have that with anyone else.

That's what I was thinking when Nadia and I said our sorries. Jules walked over at the end of our apology fest.

He looked super cute that day. He had on a blue Popeye T-shirt. The blue matched his eyes. Those eyes looked closely at me, and only at me – even though Nadia perked up at his approach. Shoulders back, chest out.

Anyway, the sorries were done. But they were like the tip of the iceberg. I'd left out the most important thing. The *most*. In her email Nadia had promised to take care of me. It made me want to scream, that line.

Because I didn't want to be taken care of. I still don't.

I close the lid of my laptop.

I am sixteen years old, and so far my thrilling weekend has consisted of a seven-year-old's birthday party, a trip to the supermarket, four DVDs, three packets of chips (two barbeque and one salt and vinegar) and one outing to the tip with dad.

Cutting edge.

It's Sunday afternoon. I sit on my bed and paint my toenails black. Three coats.

I wonder what Nadia and the gang are doing. I go on Facebook to find out.

It seems they're going to see a movie. They're going to *hear* a movie. It's American so it won't have subtitles.

They only ever chose foreign movies with subtitles so I could go with them.

I remember reading about a gadget that some inventor has created – a subtitle screen that clips on to a pair of glasses. But it won't be available for a while yet. I'll probably be old and grey by the time you can get it.

I think about texting Nadia anyway. Just in case they haven't left yet.

I miss Nadia. I miss hanging out at her house. I miss doing our biology homework together, even though it was usually me who did most of it. Nadia's job was to bring me biscuits and hot chocolates to keep me going. I can almost see the two of us sitting on her bed, food and homework between us.

I can visualise her room down to the tiny details. Her doona cover that's spotty on one side, stripy on the other. The cupboard door that's always open because of the sheer volume of crap inside it – stuff she's had since she was a baby, that Nads refuses to go through and sort out. The two photo-booth pics of us making faces that's stuck on the drawer of her messy bedside table.

I have the third photo in my room.

If I texted her now she'd probably give up going to the movie with the others. She'd come over, for me.

But I don't want that. What I want is our old friendship.

The one we had before I went deaf.

I. Don't. Want. To. Be. Taken. Care. Of.

I scroll through the contacts list in my phone. E for Erica. K for Keisha. I wonder if Keisha found a dress like the one she wanted.

I *could* text them. I could find out what they're doing today. But I haven't known them long. I don't want them to think I'm a desperate loner.

So I spend the whole afternoon studying. Five hours. And I realise I'm looking forward to going to school tomorrow.

That's how tragic my life has become.

chapter 11

Keisha and Erica wave me over to sit with them in home group. But I still need to be by the door. It's nice that they slide their books along the table and join me.

'We didn't find anything at Northfield,' Erica signs.

I flinch at the mention of that place. But I remember to breathe. I keep it together.

'But then we went into town and found two dresses. A red one and a blue one that matches Luke's eyes,' she stirs. She uses Luke's deaf name, and I know it well by now. It's the footy sign and mouthing 'Luke'.

She's in the middle of the sign when Keisha slaps her hands. I smile, but it also reminds me of Nadia, of how we used to be. She was a slapper. I can still almost feel the metal of her signet ring on my arm as she backhanded me for some comment I'd made. After I went deaf she stopped doing it, as though I was too fragile. It's a weird thing to miss.

'The dresses were only twenty dollars each,' Keisha continues, post slap.

'So we had ten dollars left over ...'

'For KFC.'

They finish each other's sentences too. It sometimes used to annoy me when Nadia did that. It would seem like a gift now.

Helena arrives. Today she is wearing long lace-up boots, and her dance routine is thumpier than it was in the ballet flats. She hands out a permission form for an excursion to the careers expo, and then goes back to the whiteboard to write down extra details. When she's finished, she unrolls a poster and tacks it to the wall.

I recognise the poster from my old school. It was stuck up in the year eleven and twelve common room, above the sandwich press. There are photos of students chatting to people at booths set up by different unis and organisations. I wonder how we're going to get the information. I wonder whether we will take along an interpreter, or whether the expo will provide one for us. Or whether we'll be expected to go it alone.

The biggest booth pictured is for the University of Melbourne. It's where I want to go. I focus on it and I'm *trying* to be positive but the doubts keep seeping in. It's as though that stupid Maggie woman from Harry's party is inside my head. *Oh really? How very brave.*

It takes a lot of effort to get her out of my head. To keep my old dream alive. There *might* be someone there who will tell me that of course I can do it. Someone other than my family who can believe in me, who can help me to believe in myself.

I'm staring at the poster as though it will give me the answers. It takes me a moment to realise that Keisha and Erica are out of their seats, pushing past me to get to the door. Everyone else in the room is looking over at the door too.

I turn to see what's going on. Keisha and Erica are hugging someone, and the someone is eclipsed by them. When they finally step aside, I see the hug-ee.

Her hair is white blonde with dark roots. It's spiky at the top, and then snakes into a long plait. It must be a hair extension, because the plait doesn't quite match the texture of the hair at the top. But it definitely looks like it's been designed that way. Nothing about this girl looks accidental.

She is small and thin and about my age, but she's not wearing a uniform. Her white T-shirt is tight, with the words 'Rage against Audism' in black across her chest.

I've never seen that word before. I don't know what it means, but the first part of the word is probably from 'audio' and the second seems a bit like 'racism', so I'm guessing that it's something to do with discrimination against deaf people.

She's wearing a low-slung studded belt, and her black jeans are frayed and ripped, exposing tartan tights underneath.

Her boots are tartan too, laces undone. When she turns around, I can see that she has a large camera strung over her shoulder.

Her brown eyes land on me, but they don't seem to register anything. For a second, I wonder if I'm actually here.

Helena drums her boots again. Her writing on the whiteboard is next to the info about the careers expo. But the style is very different. The lettering is huge and red, like a celebration.

WELCOME BACK STELLA!!!

Stella looks at the writing. She smiles at Helena and claps her hands together as she walks to the front of the room.

'Why no school uniform?' Helena signs. The rest of us are the audience.

'I'm jet-lagged,' Stella signs back, her hand flying across her front like a plane. She doesn't voice as she signs. 'I just came in to get books so I can do my homework.'

'Weren't you … take books with you? Weren't you … to be studying while you were away?' Helena quizzes. I figure out the missing bit means something like 'supposed to' or 'going to'. I'm getting faster at this.

'I was studying,' Stella signs, head tilted. 'I was right in the middle of the school of life.' The word 'middle' is emphasised, Stella's right hand chopping heavily down on her left.

The performance is mesmerising. I glance around the

room and see that the others are also staring with what looks like awe. Luke has his chin in his hands as he looks at Stella. I wonder whether she has been the cause of one of his past heartbreaks. Keisha's eyes move between Luke and Stella, and I wish Luke would see Keisha properly, would notice how she looks at him. Everything could be so easy and un-heartbreaking.

The three kids in front of me lean forward, enjoying uninterrupted views of the Stella show.

Helena rolls her eyes exaggeratedly. She bites down on her smile and hands a form to Stella. 'We have an excursion to the careers expo Wednesday week,' she signs to Stella. 'I think you will be interested. So I hope we will have the pleasure of your company.'

Stella shrugs, like the expo is no biggie. I have a feeling she already knows where her future lies.

Helena shoos us out of the classroom the way she always does when it's time to move to the next class. I've grown used to it. I actually kind of like the way she does it. It's clear and predictable and familiar. Like she knows us all well enough to 'shoo'.

I stay seated for a minute as everyone leaves. I feel new all over again. As in, awkwardly new. It's weird, because before Stella arrived this morning, I'd been thinking how nice it was to have started feeling settled in.

I'm right near the door as usual, so everyone has to pass me. When Stella passes, I can't help checking to see whether she has hearing aids or a cochlear. It's become a habit when I'm around deaf people, searching for an indication of whether someone can hear anything at all.

It's not like I'm staring. More like I'm sneaking a look. I am leaning against my hand, and only my eyes travel.

But it seems that she's caught me anyway. Her eyes make a quick assessment. She blinks, and it feels like she has taken a mental snapshot of me to study later. But that's ridiculous. It's probably just me being paranoid.

As I stand up I see Keisha, Erica, Luke, Cameron and Stella all gathered just outside the door. Their signing is fast and furious and I only catch words here and there. They obviously have a lot to catch up on.

Erica beckons for me to join them. I point to my homework. We have English next. I finished my essay on *A Thing of Beauty* last night, but I need an excuse. For some reason I'm not quite ready to be with them.

I watch them walk off. They have made a formation around Stella, two devotees on each side. The shape means that everyone can address Stella, everyone can see what she's saying.

Stella is very definitely at the centre.

I need to swim after school. I'm in a funny mood. Unsettled, and I know it's about Stella even though that's dumb. She made such a brief appearance today, and I don't know why she had such an impact.

But I'm kind of nervy, like Stella's arrival may have changed the dynamics of the group. I'm not sure where I'll fit now that she's back.

I go into the change room, and I hold my towel around me as I change. Then I put my swimming cap on and take a quick glance at myself in the mirror. My head looks like a bright yellow egg. The cap pinches a bit of skin on my forehead, but I don't adjust it yet. I back out of the change room, dragging all my stuff from school.

I've forgotten that the lockers are so close, and I bang into them. I forget how much sound that would make. Is it more reverberation than loud sound? I hope so. They are old lockers, fastened to each other but not to the wall. There is definitely a bit of wobble. Enough wobble to destabilise someone crouching down in front of the lockers.

It's a boy, wearing the purple and navy speedos of the swimming squad that often train here. He looks about my age. His shoulders are broad and impressive. He says something. I can only see the side of his mouth moving, but it's pretty obvious he's swearing. He's sitting on the concrete floor because I've made him lose balance and fall.

I say a quick sorry, eager to be away from him, to be in the pool and anonymous.

He stands up. There's a lot of him, standing up. He turns and looks at me. I feel extra conscious of my egg head. But I can't help looking at him. His eyes are green, almost exactly the same colour as mine, though his hair is as blond as mine is dark.

'It's OK,' he says. 'You're OK. I've just … one of … crap –'

He's losing me. He is not looking directly at me anymore, and it's too hard. I could stop him. I could ask him to look at me when he's talking because I'm deaf. I could say that to every new person I meet. But I won't, I don't, so I walk away.

I don't want to negotiate getting a locker with him there. I realise with horror that I'm standing right under the disabled sign of the change room behind me.

My own personalised backdrop. *Check out the handicapped girl!*

I need to get away. I dump my stuff on one of the chairs next to the pool and dive in.

chapter 12

The next morning everyone is ushered into the school hall. It's dark, except for a large lit rectangle projected on the wall above the podium.

I sit at the end of the row, nearest the door.

Erica and Keisha squeeze past me, and then Luke and Cam fill up the next two spaces. I notice that Keisha has managed to get a seat next to Luke, and I feel good for her. Just having him next to her makes her beam. I lean forward and smile at her.

The art teacher, a woman called Juanita, is waiting up the front. Just standing there, she isn't getting anyone's attention. The hall is a mass of moving hands as kids sign and muck around.

Eventually Juanita resorts to the light switch system, flicking them on and off.

'This morning we are lucky to share in a student's assessment task for art,' she signs when the hall calms down. She has huge, expressive hands. It's like you couldn't look anywhere else if you tried. There's a theatrical slant to her signing of the word art. It makes me want to know what it is she's painting when she brushes one thumb down the other hand's palm.

'I am sure you'll agree that S-t-e-l-l-a has created something memorable. It's not finished, but it's particularly special because it relates to all of us here at the College for the Deaf.'

Stella walks up the stairs and over to the podium. She is in school uniform but at first glance I don't quite believe that she's wearing the whole thing. But when I check each bit off mentally – dress, jumper, white socks, black shoes – she totally is.

I guess it's her hair and her make-up that makes her look different, or like she isn't really in uniform. She has bobby-pinned bits of her hair into a whole lot of little twirls on top of her head. Her eyes are rimmed so heavily with eyeliner that I can see it from here.

Stella doesn't say, or sign, anything. She just presses a button on the digital projector.

A photo fills the white space on the wall. It's of a group of kids on an oval. They seem to be playing with a ball, but it's not a regular ball. It looks like a glass bubble. It takes me a second to notice that there's a girl inside the bubble, looking out. Her hands are pressed against the surface of the ball.

A few metres away a little boy is standing with one foot out, getting ready to kick the ball. And, I guess, the little girl inside.

The bubble is Stella's constant theme, and it's clear what it represents. Deafness. Isolation. It's used in every photo, but in different ways and different situations. Each photo is amazing. I am frozen to my seat.

The next photo is of a girl, a teenager. She's beautiful. She is wearing a purple dress, sort of floaty, and black boots. She is sitting cross-legged in front of the camera. She's also inside a bubble. One of her arms is folded around her waist, the other is raised so that her hand goes up to her chin. It's a contemplative look, but it's also more than that. Her eyes are downcast, her lips follow the same lines.

Maybe it's because the girl is about my age, but this photo draws me in even more than the others. There's a stillness about it that becomes more disturbing as I stare at it. It's as though it's not only her body, but also her thoughts and feelings that are trapped inside the bubble.

Next is a photo of a man. He has a metal band around his ankle, a chain leading from it. At the end of the chain is a bubble. It makes me think of a prisoner's ball and chain from the olden days. The man is dragging his foot behind him, obviously struggling with the weight of the bubble. It's as though he's dragging his deafness behind him like a punishment. In the corner of the frame stands a man in a blue uniform.

He wore a blue uniform. The brick of a guard at Northfield. Stella has brought it all back to me, and it's like she's found a brand new copy of that worn out memory and pressed the play button.

I'd been shopping. I had my bags and was walking out of some jeans shop. I was thinking about the very cool but very expensive jeans I'd just tried on when someone pushed past me, running. I only saw the back of her so I didn't see who it was, but she was wearing the same school uniform as me. I didn't think anything of it, and just kept walking.

Suddenly, from nowhere, there were two huge, heavy hands pressing on my shoulders. I jumped in fright, my heart hammering. My bags flew everywhere as I tried to swing around but it was hopeless. The hands held me tight, and with another wave of panic I realised that he was so strong I didn't stand a chance.

I had no idea what was going on. Zero. Maybe he was a rapist? A serial killer? I was so freaked out that it didn't even occur to me that a rapist probably wouldn't try to grab someone in the middle of a busy shopping centre.

My breathing was shallow and fast and I remember wondering if I was having a heart attack or something, even though I don't know any normal teenagers who have heart attacks out of the blue. I didn't think I'd have enough breath to scream, or if I did manage to make a noise I don't think it would have been very loud.

I felt my legs buckle, and as I collapsed to the ground like a rag doll I knew people were staring. I thought I was going to black out. I wasn't worried about the serial killer anymore because surely all these people wouldn't just stand there and watch me being attacked.

I was worried about embarrassing myself. I knew now what was happening, because it wasn't the first time. But it was the first time in public. Behold, the Public Panic Attack. I was the freak star. But wait, there was more. When I finally drew breath, they got a panicked, screaming deaf girl for the same price (free). I can only imagine what the sounds I was making would have been like.

It seemed like years before I realised he was a security guard. Years more before I found out that the store's buzzer had gone off and the girl who pushed past me had probably stolen something.

Afterwards he took me to the centre's management. They apologised. They offered to call my parents. I said no.

I didn't want Mum and Dad to know what had happened. I didn't want anyone to know what had happened. Ever.

I take a ragged breath and I'm back in the school hall, surrounded by other kids, looking at Stella's photos.

I've been doing well. Really well. I nearly had that attack in front of Erica and Keisha but I stopped it. I've never spoken about it to anyone but it's like Stella knows about it, somehow. I feel like this girl I don't even know has invaded my privacy, exposed my nightmare-memory.

I feel like I'm pinned up on that wall at the front of the hall, for everyone to stare at.

I am at the end of the row. If I got up and left, would people notice? I remind myself to breathe, but it's hard to get enough air.

Everyone is intent on watching Stella's slides. At least no-one is looking at me. But I don't want to watch anymore. I close my eyes until she's shown all her photos and it's over. Finally.

At lunchtime we sit at the usual table, but it's different. For starters, there's a whole pile of food in the middle of the table from the food tech students, who've used stuff from the veggie garden.

And for seconds, of course, there's Stella.

'That photo session was deep,' Cam signs. The 'deep' sign is like a finger gun, dropping down. Cam makes his finger gun drop dramatically until it disappears under the table. It would have been funny if I was in the mood for funny.

I watch for Stella's reaction. Her eye-rolling is impressive, especially with the eyeliner. I have a feeling that her don't-mess-with-me look would beat mine, hands down. The beginnings of it seem stuck to her face permanently.

Erica and Stella start signing about the techniques Stella used in her photos. Keisha frowns, obviously not following.

'It was deep,' Keisha signs enthusiastically, during a break in their signing. 'But I don't think I really got it.'

Stella pauses, and I can see her thinking about how she should explain the photos for Keisha.

'My photos are a commentary on how the hearies treat us,' she signs.

When Stella makes the sign for 'hearies', it's harsh. The sign for hearing is the index finger travelling from ear to mouth. Everything functioning. In Stella's version though, her index finger and little finger stick up like devil's ears as she makes the sign. As a final flourish, she blows on her fingers, like she's blowing out a candle. It's a dismissive gesture. It seems to say 'they know nothing'.

I don't like her version of the sign. It feels rude, like she's suggesting that hearing people are the enemy, or evil somehow. Once I might have called her on it. But I'm not up for a debate with Stella. So I just watch.

'Right,' Keisha says slowly, though I'm not sure she has got Stella's point. 'But how did you get the people inside the bubbles?'

The others laugh. I even smile a bit.

'Remember when I said we should take iced water to the school sports in year seven?' Luke signs, looking at Keisha.

Cam joins in. 'And Chatter told him not to be silly because we wouldn't be able to get ice into the bottle?'

The boys crack up. Keisha screws up her nose. I think she might still be wondering how you get ice into a bottle.

'I made the bubble digitally', Stella signs, pushing Cam back so that Keisha can see her. 'Then I photoshopped the people in or around it.'

'That's one way of doing it,' Luke signs from across the table. 'Or you could shrink someone, turn them into liquid and blow them into the bubble through a straw.'

Keisha pokes out her tongue at Luke, and I notice that he grins and grabs her hand.

I pick up a piece of quiche and take a bite. The centre is a bit eggy, not quite cooked. I'm deciding whether to have another bite when Stella looks right at me.

'You're new,' she signs.

I feel some egg slip down my throat.

'Yeah. I started last week,' I sign, voicing as well. I wipe some quiche from my lip.

'You're oral,' Stella signs, and there's a disapproving look in her eyes, though I guess I might just have egg on my lip.

It's only now that I realise no-one has been speaking today. I'm getting so used to any combination of sign and speaking that it doesn't always register anymore.

'D-e-m-i has only been deaf for two years,' Erica steps in, and I feel like she's offering a defence for me, somehow. 'But she signs really well. She's improved heaps since she's been here.'

'So new, so hot,' Luke signs to Stella, like I'm not sitting right there. Keisha shifts in her seat. I wish Luke would just stop, but he doesn't. 'She's already broken my heart.'

Stella laughs, and when she does, her face completely changes. It's like something opens inside of her.

'Good work, D-e-m-i,' she signs. 'In record time too. Good to get that over with.'

chapter 13

After school, Keisha begs me to go and watch Luke play footy at the high school next door. She doesn't want to go alone, and Erica has something on. I'm not a big footy fan, but I don't have anything else to do, other than more homework.

It's purple-blazer territory around the sidelines of the oval. We put our bags on a row of seats.

Keisha waves, and I look over to where her wave is directed. Luke is with a group of boys all gathered around their footy coach. The coach is waving his arms around, and I think he's probably yelling.

We leave our bags on the seats next to the oval and walk a bit closer to the action.

From here, I can see Luke straining to follow what the coach is talking about. I can see him focusing on the coach's lips. When the coach moves his head sideways, Luke leans sideways a bit so he doesn't lose sight of the coach's mouth. My head leans with him, as though I can help. But I am pretty sure he'd be missing a lot. Luke is profoundly deaf, like me. He looks like he's trying to fill in the gaps of understanding, and I know what that means. I know how big some of the gaps can be.

I think Luke's brave, doing this. Being the only one in the team who can't hear. I look at Keisha and see she is obviously feeling an exaggerated version of what I'm feeling. Her head is tilted sideways, her eyes are wide and her right hand is crossed over her heart, as though she's holding it in place.

The boys run onto the field in a pack of purple, navy and yellow. The other team runs on too, in red and white jerseys. The umpire bounces the ball and it's game on.

Keisha and I walk back to the seats. Although most of the rows are empty, our bags have been dumped on the ground. Sitting in the seat where my bag used to be is Horse Girl. She is with another girl, but I don't think it's one from my tram.

She stares at me as I approach. I can feel her eyes scanning me, from top to toe. I don't like it. I don't like her. It's as though we are two animals with opposing scents. I reach down and pull my bag from next to her feet. She doesn't move. She doesn't make it easy.

Keisha hasn't registered anything. She just pulls her bag out from under the other girl's feet. Her eyes are locked on the oval, following Luke even when he's nowhere near the football. She walks to the end of the row and sits down. I throw my bag over one shoulder and meet her there.

'Did you see that mark?' Keisha signs. 'That was Luke. Did you see it? He's really good. How high did he jump?'

Her questions are rhetorical. I nod, because that's all that's required. I sneak a look towards the girls. Horse Girl points two handed, as though one isn't enough, in the direction of our school. Our DEAF school.

Then, she keeps her hands in the air. She is mimicking Keisha. Her hands are flapping about in the air, hitting each other and doing air circles. The gestures are ridiculous. They are nothing like sign. They mean nothing. They mean nothing except that she thinks that's how sign language looks. Retarded.

The girl with her shakes her head, but she is struggling to control her giggles. I can tell she is finding Horse Girl's antics guiltily amusing.

I feel sick. Keisha hasn't noticed anything. She's deep in a Luke-trance.

I look at the ground. I breathe. There is nothing I can do about her. Nothing.

If I went up and tried to talk to her, what would I say? 'Don't be mean to us poor deaf kids'? Besides, even if I did that, she would hear me speak, which would be a bonus for her. She'd find that extra funny. Something else to mimic for everyone's enjoyment.

There's no point in making myself – us – a bigger target.

There's nothing I can do except to breathe my humiliation right down to the pit of my stomach.

Now Keisha looks in the direction of Horse Girl and her friend. The two of them are walking away.

For a second, I wonder whether Keisha has seen it. Her eye-roll tells me she has. But it's an eye-roll that says 'how annoying,' not 'how humiliating, I want to die'. She has seen Horse Girl imitating her signing, and it's hardly had any effect.

Maybe that's how you get if you've been deaf forever? Maybe she's put up with rudeness so many times that now it's no big deal? Maybe I'll get used to stuff like that one day?

I doubt it. I don't think I even want to, although it would probably be less painful.

I'm thinking about all this when Keisha suddenly waves her hand in my face. It's so close I can feel the breeze she makes.

'Luke's been hurt!' she signs. Now she *is* upset. Her hand flies to her mouth.

I look out at the players on the oval. 'What happened?' I ask.

'Luke took a mark, and that other guy tried to stop him, and gave him a blood nose!'

The match has stopped. Luke is heading back to the

sidelines holding his nose. He's walking over with another player from his team.

'That's him! The guy who hurt Luke! Bastard!' Her hands are fists, the little finger edges bumping each other violently, twice, to make the 'bastard' sign.

I look around to see if anyone is watching us. It doesn't seem like it, but I turn towards Keisha, blocking out the people in the stands, just in case.

'It must have been an accident,' I sign. 'They're on the same team.'

I can see Keisha taking it in, her anger changing into concern. Her face is easy to read – an open book.

'It doesn't look serious,' I continue, hands tucked close to my chest so as not to be too obvious.

But Keisha isn't concentrating on me. She's watching the coach hand Luke an ice-pack. I flinch as Keisha starts to walk over to them. I think she should back off a bit. Maybe try not to be so obvious where Luke's concerned. I stay where I am but my eyes follow her. I look at the 'bastard' who bumped into Luke.

It's Swimming Guy.

I shut my eyes, plead with the universe. I don't want to be the girl from the deaf school. I don't want to be deaf.

When I open my eyes, three pairs of feet are walking towards me. Keisha's. Luke's. And his.

I am still deaf.

Keisha is walking between the boys, smiling. She's obviously reconsidered her opinion about Swimming Guy being a bastard, but I kind of want him to be one so I don't have to care what happens. So I don't have to stand there and go through the clunk of him finding out that I'm deaf. His expression of sympathy, of pity.

I don't suppose he'll remember me. I'm not sure if I want him to. I could still walk away, but Keisha is signing to me as they approach so it would be rude.

'It was an accident!' she signs, as though she's delivering a great revelation instead of stating the obvious. 'They went up for the same mark, and sometimes that happens in football.'

I nod. There's still a bit of blood around his nose but other than that, Luke looks fine.

Keisha pulls out her mobile and types.

Demi, Ethan.

His eyes move from the screen to me. And they kind of *catch* me. I know that eyes can't catch, but his do somehow. And straight away, I can tell that he recognises me. His eyes widen slightly, almond-shaped becoming circular. And there's a smile tugging at the edges of his mouth.

Then I see him registering that I'm deaf. But if most people gulp down that realisation, he seems to sip it. It's different to what I expected. To what I'd feared. If he feels sorry for me, I can't see any evidence of it.

'Be careful,' Luke is more miming than signing to Ethan. The 'careful' is a shake of his index finger. 'She's hot and she'll break your heart'. That's done with Luke pointing directly at me, then blowing on the same finger. Then he places his hands on his heart and pulls them apart melodramatically.

Keisha slaps him on the shoulder and I hope it hurts. I am horrified. I don't know where to look. But Swimming Guy is laughing.

His name is Ethan, and he is laughing and his green eyes are smiling and he doesn't *look* like he feels sorry for me.

'Yeah, I'd better be careful,' he says, and I can read those lips pretty well. I can put together what he's saying. 'She does ... dangerous. She looks ... the kind of girl ... over a locker.'

Luke and Keisha have no clue what he's on about. They turn and start signing about football and Luke's nose and who knows what else.

And I'm glad. I'm glad that Ethan remembers me, and I'm glad that it's only him and me sharing this joke.

It's not much, I tell myself, and it's true. Not much has happened. But even as I tell myself that, I think about swimming next to him, our bodies in perfect sync. I wonder what that means. I have a nagging, silly hope that it means something and now I'm flustered and I think I might be going red.

'I've got to go,' I say to him, and I just have to hope my voice sounds normal.

I didn't think I would like anyone ever again, not after what happened with Jules. In fact I made it a *rule* not to. But it seems it's true. All rules have exceptions.

chapter 14

By the time I get home, my thoughts have turned sour. It's like Horse Girl is inside my head, feeding me lines.

As if. As if. He's not only normal, he's gorgeous. And you? You are a deaf girl who goes to a weird deaf school.

I try to shove nasty Horse Girl thoughts out of my head. I don't want her to be in my head, in my bedroom. But I keep seeing the way she stared at Keisha and me as though we were freaks. The way she pointed to the deaf school, two handed, as though pointing to a very different planet.

As though we shouldn't be at the footy, and we *should* be stuck in a bubble somewhere away from normal people, like in Stella's photos.

I have another nagging feeling. At least at my old school I was mixing with hearing people. That would seem more normal to someone like Ethan. The feeling grows when I think about my old gang, especially about Nadia.

I feel like half of me is missing without Nadia around every day, being annoying, or even taking care of me, if that's what it would take to keep us close.

My school work has improved since I started at the

deaf school – I'm understanding nearly everything in class. But life isn't all about school work. Maybe I've made the wrong decision?

I thought I was past all this doubt. I need to remind myself that my decision wasn't only to do with school work. It was about the rest of my life too. I mustn't get too romantic about my old school. Things had changed. I didn't really *fit* in there anymore, even when I thought I did. Even when I thought I passed for being normal, I was kidding myself.

I guess it's kind of like being homesick for your old house when it's been pulled down and replaced with a block of flats. It's not there anymore; you can't go back. But you still miss it somehow.

There is a DVD disc with an ordinary printed label in the right-hand drawer of my bedside table. Speech Night. It looks innocent. My TV is on the wall. Around the edges are stickers, and the third photo booth pic of me and Nads.

Maybe I want to punish myself for dreaming of a normal life, a normal boyfriend. I don't really know what makes me decide to watch it again, but I push the disc in the slot.

The first time I watched it, I was tucked under my doona with a bowl of popcorn on my bedside table.

Now, I sit on the end of the bed. No snacks. No doona.

The beginning of the DVD is jumpy. The media students had been practising their skills at cutting between cameras.

The first bit shows people in the audience taking their seats. There's a pan of the auditorium roof, then the camera comes down to the stage.

There's more stability as Olivia sidles up to the microphone. There are closed captions at the bottom of the screen, just for me since there were no other deaf students. As Olivia speaks, her words appear on the screen below.

The time limit for each speech is two minutes. All of us have chosen a topic around the environment. Olivia talks about climate change and the debate about its scientific link to greenhouse gas emissions.

The camera scans the audience as everyone claps at the end of the talk. I see Mum, Dad and Harry sitting in their seats. Harry is clapping along, being very grown-up, his little face all serious. Oscar is squirming around on Felicity's lap, trying to lock his chubby legs into a standing position.

The camera cuts back to the stage as Justin comes on. It's typical Justin. He's wearing the usual short-sleeved white shirt and tie but he has ditched the blazer and the shirt is about two sizes too small.

When Justin starts talking about an emissions trading scheme, I know to look at the kids in the corner of the screen, just off to the left-hand side. I know that *this time*. It's a parallel narrative there, more telling than what's on centre stage.

As Justin talks, Liam, the class clown, flexes his muscles, posing like a body builder. I can't tell which kids are with him. It's too shadowy. But I can see their shoulders shaking, and it's clear they're laughing at Liam's take-off.

The first time I watched the DVD, I laughed too. I laughed at the way Liam caught the gist of Justin's vanity. I laughed at the way Liam played with what was happening onstage. Each of Justin's arm movements looked like it was showing off an impressive muscle group rather than explaining the impact of dangerous emissions. I laughed with a mouthful of popcorn. I had to sip my drink to avoid choking.

I'm not laughing now. I know what's coming.

I watch myself walk out onstage after Justin finishes.

It's obvious that I'm nervous. My footsteps are clumsy, as though my school shoes are made of concrete and my arms are pinned unnaturally to my side. I remember reassuring myself that I knew my speech, word for word, and I can almost see myself breathing in that reassurance.

The back of Jules' head appears at the bottom of the screen, standing to the right of the stage on the ground. I cringe as I watch the screen-Demi deliberately *not* looking at Jules, trying to be independent of him after what happened at the market.

I see myself looking straight into the auditorium, remembering my teacher's advice to talk to the back of the room so that everyone would be able to hear me.

Screen-Demi leans into the microphone. *I* lean into the microphone and start my speech.

My words appear across the bottom of the screen, line by line, like karaoke. I can see the writing, but it's not the words I focus on now. Jules is in view again. It's still just the back of him, standing up, but I can see what he's doing, though of course I didn't see it at the time.

I can see it all too clearly – now. His hands are in front of him, and are pushing down. It's an easy sign, one of the first I learnt. He's telling me to lower my volume.

I have to be tough with myself. I have to keep watching.

There's no point trying to warn screen-Demi to look at Jules.

My eyes switch to the left side of the screen, to Liam and the other kids in the shadows. Liam is covering his ears with his hands, shaking his head from side to side as though he's being rocked by some earsplitting noise. I know the kids near Liam are laughing because I can see their shoulders shaking. Again. This time though, they're laughing at the poor deaf girl making a fool of herself.

Get it now on DVD!

I turn off the TV, and I switch off the silly idea that Ethan might like me. That something might happen between us.

As if.

chapter 15

I catch the early tram the next morning. We have the excursion to the careers expo this afternoon. I left my university course handbook at school and I want to use it to prepare some questions.

And I want to avoid Horse Girl.

There are no free seats. The tram is packed and I have to stand and hold onto a handle. I keep thinking of Ethan, despite trying to switch off any thoughts about him last night. His shoulders, his arms, his green eyes and the way he looked at me. I should probably stop myself, but I don't want to. At least I can daydream about him.

My phone vibrates in my pocket. I lurch forward as the tram stops and juggle my phone out of my pocket. It's a text from Keisha.

Ethan asked for yr phone # after u left.

I study the message like it might rewrite itself or disappear unless my eyes keep it pinned to the screen. My heart flies up to my throat as I frantically text back.

What did u do?

Commuters push past me as we approach a popular stop. My phone vibrates in my hand, but I have to let some people past before I can look at the new message.

I feel a nervous, strange fluttering inside me. I get a flash of Horse Girl making fun of Keisha and me at the football. But Ethan has asked for my phone number, even though he knows.

It's scary, but I hope Keisha gave my number to him.

I miss out on so much. I don't want to miss out on this too.

I told him yr gay.

I drop my arm down from the handle, and it's silly how the panic rises in me. I'm taken by surprise when the tram lurches off again.

U didn't? Did u???

I wait for the vibration of the response. It seems to take ages.

Nup. I told him u have a b'friend.

I resend my last message.

U didn't? Did u???
Nup.
Did u give it to him???
Gtg. Tell u at school x

It's quiet at school. There are a few smaller kids mucking around on the play equipment. A little girl waves to me. I wave back, smiling. It feels like it's going to be a good day.

I get the uni handbook from my locker. The homeroom is unlocked. I sit down and try to organise my preferences for courses. It feels like a game, like a kid's wishlist for Santa or something, instead of a real list of course preferences. My first preference is law at Melbourne.

My first preference is Ethan.

I shake my head and try to concentrate. Out of the corner of my eye I see Helena walk in. She is talking into her streamer. She waves at me and continues her conversation. I hope I don't seem weird, but I still can't help staring at

Helena when she uses her streamer. I try to imagine what it would be like to be able to do what she's doing right now. But even though I wish I could use a streamer, I can't really be jealous of her. She's too nice.

'Hi,' she signs to me after she's finished. She sits down next to me. 'That was my daughter. She forgot her lunch.'

'I didn't know you have a daughter,' I sign back.

'I have two,' she signs, 'A-p-r-i-l is six and G-o-l-d-i-e is four.'

'Nice names,' I sign. It feels good to be sitting here just with her, finding out about her life outside school.

'Are they – '

Suddenly, I'm not sure if I should be asking the question, but Helena answers immediately.

'No, they're both hearing,' she signs, as though the question is not only reasonable but to be expected. 'My husband is profoundly deaf, and I'm partially deaf. We all sign, and three of us speak, so we're a mixed mob.'

I like the idea of Helena and her mixed mob. It *must* work, at least some of the time. Even though Helena has some hearing, her husband is like me. It's not *exactly* the same as it would be, could be, with Ethan, but it still gives me hope.

'What about you, D-e-m-i?' she signs.

'No-one else in my family is deaf. Mum's a pretty good signer, my sister's OK, and Dad's not so great.'

I feel a bit bad saying that about Dad. Because even though he's not a great signer, we still seem to be able to communicate better than I do with Mum and Flawless.

'But they all give it a go?' prompts Helena. 'That's good. It's different for everyone. Stella's whole family is deaf, so sign is their first language, but you know Chatter only has her Mum, and she hardly knows any sign at all.'

'Wow. No, I didn't know that.'

It's hard to imagine what that might be like for Keisha, living alone with a mum who can't sign. Keisha's never mentioned it, in all her constant chatter.

Students are filtering in now, and Helena gets up and walks to her desk.

Erica comes in first and sits next to me. A minute later Keisha slides in next to her. I'm wishing Keisha had got here first because I want to find out what actually happened yesterday, and whether she gave Ethan my phone number.

All I get from her is a funny grin that could mean anything.

Stella, Luke and Cameron take the seats in front of us. Stella glances back quickly, looking at me and then at the door. She tilts her head and smiles at me. I have a funny, flighty sense that she might have figured out that I always sit by the door, but she could just be smiling, I guess.

'OK, everyone,' Helena signs after getting our attention with her regular routine, 'I hope you all have questions prepared, and a list of booths you would like to visit. Make sure you double-check which subjects you'll need to take next year, and the scores you'll need for any courses you're interested in. They can change from year to year.'

'Luke,' continues Helena, signing Luke's deaf name with the football sign, 'what's your plan?'

It seems natural for Helena to use Luke's deaf name. When Alistair does it, it seems kind of awkward, strained. Helena's the only teacher who really gets away with it.

'There is a TAFE booth I want to visit,' Luke signs. 'I'd like to finish this year here, and go there for year twelve. But I also want to check out whether it's OK to get my own carpentry apprenticeship lined-up while I do TAFE because I have a family friend who has offered me one.'

'Great,' Helena signs. 'What about you, C-a-m?'

'I have to line-up my preferences for accounting,' Cam signs. 'There are two different courses. I already pretty much know what's involved because Dad's an accountant.'

There's a look of distaste on Cam's face, a slight screwing up of his nose. I wonder whether his personality will go with the job.

'Or I might just be a pro surfer,' he signs with a grin, confirming my thoughts.

'Got to learn to stand up on the board for that,' Luke stirs.

Cam gives him the 'up yours' sign behind his handbook.

'Star?' I get a strange feeling when Helena uses Stella's deaf name. It shows a closeness between them that makes me kind of jealous.

'I am going to G-a-l-l-a-u-d-e-t University. I am going to study photography and then I am going to take photos that matter. I want to take photos that highlight the deaf community and put us on everyone's radar. Today I want to just check the courses here, though they won't be as good.'

Helena nods, impressed. 'G-a-l-l-a-u-d-e-t University, for those of you who don't know, is the world's only university for the deaf.'

I am in the don't-know camp.

'It's in Washington D.C. Star has only just come back from there, haven't you?'

Stella nods. 'And it was awesome,' she signs.

I'm not feeling very impressive after Stella's little speech. She seems so focused, so determined. And so do the others I guess, in their own way.

But the careers they're interested in seem more realistic than law. I can't see that many problems in being a deaf carpenter or a deaf accountant.

And it's quite realistic to want to become a photographer

when you're deaf. You could work alone. Even if I did become a lawyer, I don't know how I could actually work in a regular courtroom system. I've told myself to take one step at a time, but sometimes I feel that the next step will be right into a black hole.

I hope Helena grills someone else. For once the universe grants my wish. She does. 'Chatter?'

'I want to be famous.' The sign for famous is like two little birds flying away from each eyebrow. Keisha flies her hands really high.

'Oh, really,' Helena signs with a smile. 'What would you like to be famous for?'

'Whatever,' Keisha replies, shrugging.

Everyone laughs, including me. But I'm glad when we run out of time.

chapter 16

Everyone is kind of red-cordial-ish on the bus to the careers expo. I think it's because we're all trying to keep hold of a bit of childhood. It's like we're all a bit freaked out that we're old enough to consider 'careers'. Hands are flying about, and I reckon if I could hear it, the laughter would have a nervous edge.

I hope we don't stand out too much at the expo. I'm worried that the others will, especially when they're all revved up like this. I might blend in OK if I don't sign too much. It's not like I have a cochlear implant or hearing aids or anything to give me away.

I am sitting by the window. Keisha is next to me. She's still joking about being famous. She plans to carry a chihuahua around in a handbag. I wouldn't be seen dead with a dog in a handbag, but it's pretty funny watching Keisha explain her plans for fame. Especially since the sign for chihuahua is so cute. It actually looks like the animal, with the middle and ring fingers touching the thumb, the index and little fingers sticking up like ears. Then you wiggle your hand in little circles.

I hope she doesn't do it too much in public, but Keisha *is* an amazing signer. And her facial expressions are so animated. She totally deserves her deaf name – it feels like ages before I get a chance to ask her about Ethan.

'So? Did you give Ethan my phone number?' I sign small and close to my chest, making sure no-one else can see.

'God, he's really hot, D,' she replies. 'Don't you think? His eyes and his hair. He's got a good body, too.'

Her shaping of Ethan's body is accurate. His broad shoulders that taper down to a narrow waist.

'Luke reckons he's the best player in the whole league! He gets best and fairest trophies all the time. But how ugly are those footy jerseys? Purple, blue and yellow. Yuk. I told Luke –'

'Chatter,' I interrupt, and I have to because Keisha can jump from subject to subject until you can't even remember where she started, 'did you give him my phone number?'

'Well, after you left, this girl came up to him. You should have seen her. She was all over him. But I don't think he likes her because he kept trying to move away from her, but she was a magnet, right back next to him. So I wasn't sure whether to give him your number in front of her. But then, I was going to go home pretty soon, so I thought to myself, you'd better just do it or –'

'Chatter!'

'What?'

'Did you give him my number?'

Keisha grins, and it's only then that I understand she's doing it on purpose. She's torturing me. I give her a sharp poke in the ribs.

'Yes!' she signs finally.

As the bus pulls into the car park, part of me is thinking, *here we go, a bunch of deaf kids getting off the special bus.* But I'm grinning anyway.

Ethan has my phone number.

Helena tells us we can wander around the expo as long as we stay in pairs. We are to meet at the entrance in two hours. She tells us to text her if we need an interpreter at any time.

I look around, wondering where to begin. There are students everywhere, milling around the booths that line the aisles. I imagine it would be noisy in here.

Luke sees a booth and heads towards it with Keisha in tow. Erica follows them. I can see Luke and Keisha's hands brushing. Then I see him taking hold of her hand.

Just like that. And I understand that something has shifted between them, and that whatever happened must have happened after footy practice.

It's gorgeous, and weird, to think something so ordinary as watching a footy practice could have turned out like this.

I look around, trying to focus. It's all a bit full-on, the booths, the options. I'm wondering if I should start at my last preference and work my way up to the Melbourne pipe dream, or the other way around.

'So, where do you want to start?' Stella signs. She has obviously decided we'll be together. Her head is tilted sideways and I realise that there's a bit of doubt in that angle.

I glance down at the guide Helena has given me. 'There's a photographic college at Booth 10.' I keep my signing small, so as not to draw attention.

'Come with me?' she signs, eyebrows raised.

Even though she's way shorter than me, Stella's strides are big. It's as though she's trying to take a shortcut into the future. I feel a little wave, like the wave of admiration for Luke coping with being the only deaf player in a footy team.

But then it occurs to me that despite all her force, all that certainty, maybe she's not quite as confident as she seems. The thoughts shift my feelings about Stella a little.

They make her seem a little less untouchable.

The guy from the photographic college wears an army shirt, an eyebrow piercing and three-day stubble. He looks the part – he's clearly an artist. He smiles as we walk towards him.

'Would you like to know a bit about our college?' he asks.

Stella is close beside me. She doesn't react. I wonder whether she's had problems lip-reading him. Just in case, I sign what he's said. I can see him registering our deafness. Despite his cool look, he seems fazed, like he's not quite sure how to continue.

'It's OK,' I tell him, 'I can lip-read.'

'Oh, good … good,' he says falteringly.

Stella shifts from foot to foot. She won't look at him. I think back to her photos of deaf people being shut out and isolated, even persecuted, and I'm pretty sure this is tough for her. It's like she's being forced to fraternise with the enemy.

'Can you ask him if they have film as well as digital classes?' Stella signs to me.

It's weird to have Stella deferring to me. She's a fish out of water here. If her whole family is deaf then she probably doesn't spend much time with hearing people like I do.

Artist Guy talks about the course, and I sign what he's

said to Stella. It's not hard to lip-read him. He's facing me, giving me his full attention. But I have to drop the idea of pretending that I'm not deaf because I need to sign what he's saying to Stella.

When other students come up to the booth, he tells them to come back in five minutes. I know it's a bit irrational, but I feel kind of annoyed when he does that. In his politeness, he's separating us from the other students. Making us special. Making us different.

We're there for way more than five more minutes. Stella barely looks at him the whole time. She just waits for me to interpret for her. It's a strange feeling, but it's actually nice to feel useful.

When she's had her fill of information, Stella just steps away from the booth. I thank the guy on her behalf.

'Thanks,' she signs as we walk away. 'Where do you want to go? You never got to say what you wanted to do after school.'

I look down at the guide. The law school from Melbourne Uni is at Booth 35, but the idea of actually going there and asking questions is suddenly daunting. It feels like I have to decide if it's a real possibility for me.

When I look at Stella, her eyebrows are still raised, impatient for my response.

'You're the smartest student in our year level, you know,' she signs.

I'm taken aback. Before I went deaf I always used to do better than my friends in tests and stuff. I was always the smart one. But my marks started slipping after I went deaf. I'm doing pretty well again now, but I didn't know that Stella had noticed. Part of me doesn't want her to, because those marks might create an expectation that I'm not sure I can fulfil.

'If you keep getting good marks next year, you could get into medicine. Or law.'

When she signs 'law' I look around to see if anyone from school has seen her. My expression must have given me away though. Stella pulls me towards Booth 35.

The woman at the booth reminds me of Maggie at Harry's party. I tell her I'm deaf and ask her a question with my voice. It's a question about entrance requirements, but I can see she's only thinking about me being deaf. She is polite and clear and I can understand her well enough, but I can see the 'how brave' stuff kicking in already. I am distracted for a moment and just catch the end of the woman saying something about *special considerations*.

She gives me a brochure and points to the website details on the back. She starts talking about all the support the uni offers.

I look down at the section of the brochure she's high-lighted. I feel my jaw clench at the words *Disability*

Liaison Unit. I scan the text and see mention of special considerations for the disabled. Unless I've misunderstood I think she's saying that the entrance requirements for disabled students – *students like me* – are different. Different to *normal* students.

I feel a flash of anger, even though the woman is smiling and being helpful.

Stella has obviously picked up on what's going on. She's looking daggers at the woman. I just want to get away from this oh-so-helpful woman and get my thoughts together. I try to smile as I put the brochure in my bag.

There's a *thwack* on my shoulder and a hand millimeters from my face. It's Keisha and Erica.

'How did you go, D?' Keisha signs. She doesn't wait for an answer. 'I can't find any courses on how to get famous!'

We all laugh.

And that's when I see them.

The old gang. Nadia, Shae, Stavros and Lockie.

They are frozen on the spot, staring at us through the crowd. And already, I'm feeling something, like I'm being split in two. The old Demi is with Nadia and the gang, watching the deaf kids. That Demi is seeing Keisha's mouth, wide open as she honks and splutters her laughter. She's watching Erica's hands as they flail around.

That Demi is noticing the exaggerated facial expressions.

She's seeing how different they are – *we* are. How *awkward* it all looks, how clumsy.

The other Demi is with her new friends, laughing – but aware, always aware, of being on the outer, of being judged by others.

When Nadia sees me looking back at her, she stops staring and waves. The gang comes towards us.

'OMG!' Nadia says. 'Demi!' Her arms are out and she grabs me and hugs. The hugs continue with the others. I'm tucked inside a cavern of hugs and I know that they're happy to see me. I try to let myself feel happy, too.

But I can feel Stella beside me. She's checking this out big time. She's watching me, she's watching my friends. I'm sure she'll think the hugs are over the top, false. Sure enough, when I glance at her, her expression is cynical. Her eyes are narrowed and she's biting her lower lip and it all seems to say, 'oh really?' As though she thinks my friends are patronising me.

It's not a comfortable feeling.

I'm kind of relieved when Stella backs away from us and removes herself from the group.

'So, who are your friends?' Nadia asks.

Her face is open and friendly, and suddenly I feel bad. Maybe I'm just being self-conscious and she wasn't thinking anything mean.

I introduce Keisha and Erica to the old gang. It's fine. Everyone is nice to each other. They talk to each other. My hearing friends make sure Erica and Keisha can see their faces as they talk about the exhibitors. My deaf friends follow the conversation. Erica is chatting away like she's known my old friends forever.

I breathe and relax, because I was wrong, wasn't I? Because my old friends aren't judgmental, and both sets of friends are good people. No-one is out to make fun of anyone.

Stavros gets out his mobile and types something on the screen. He holds it out to show me.

Small party my place fri nite. Wanna come?

It's a written confirmation of my thoughts. Everything is just fine. It's frustrating that Stella isn't here to see it.

Their teacher, one I don't know, calls the gang away. I nod and give Stavros the thumbs up as they go.

'Nice hearies,' Keisha signs.

The sign for hearies looks completely different in Keisha's hands compared to Stella's version. For one thing, Keisha is smiling. For another, she only uses her index finger and not the devil's ears that Stella uses.

I smile at Keisha. They are my friends, those hearies. They are not the enemy. They will always include me.

I turn and see Stella. She's actually only a metre or so behind me, a position that would have made it possible to read Stavros' text. I wonder if she did.

If she did, it hasn't stopped her cynical expression. It seems to have made it worse, if anything.

It's really annoying. But I decide it's best to just ignore it.

chapter 17

Ethan hasn't contacted me. He's had my number since Tuesday afternoon, now it's Thursday afternoon. I let myself stress that Keisha might have written the number down wrong or that he's lost it, but the stronger thought is that he's decided he doesn't want to contact me.

He's probably had second thoughts about seeing a deaf girl.

I walk up the street to my house. I want to have a shower, get out of my school clothes, relax.

Then I see Jules' motorbike. It's parked beside Dad's ute in the driveway.

Jesus. I don't know if I can face him yet. I still feel like an idiot after what I did. I don't think he would just turn up without being invited, so Mum will have asked him over. I'm guessing she'll have a reason.

Thanks, Mum.

I can't help walking over to his bike, lifting up the seat. There's the key, like always. Our street is pretty safe, pretty suburban, but people don't usually leave their keys in their cars or their doors unlocked.

Jules thinks that no-one will steal his bike or anything

inside the seat because *he* believes it. His ask-the-universe thing again.

And it seems the universe obeys him.

I walk down the driveway, squeezing between the house and the fence, and creep in the back door. I don't think I'm making much noise, though I have to struggle through some tree branches.

I must be doing OK because I manage to unlock the back door and get into my bedroom without anyone seeing. I even manage to get changed out of my school clothes.

I wonder what they're talking about out there?

Me, I assume.

If I go out there, at least I'll find out why he's here. But I still don't know what to say, how to explain what happened at the market.

I don't even notice my phone buzzing on the dressing table. I just check it out of habit and see I have a message. I don't recognise the number. I allow myself to hope as I open the message.

Hi Demi. I really wanted to talk to you in person, but I'm probably not going to run into you unless you go to footy practice again so I thought maybe I should text. I'm wondering if I could maybe meet you after school on Monday. I can't do tomorrow or the weekend because I'm going away with my dad,

but if you could come on Monday then maybe we could meet at the milk bar or something. Sorry it's such a long message. Oh and it's Ethan here.

It *is* a long message. I have to keep scrolling down and down. And then I have to go back up and start again. Just to check it's real.

I am being asked out. By Ethan.

I *so* don't feel like I did a minute ago. I can go out there now. I think I can even face Jules.

I don't know if I should wait before I text back, if a quick reply might show I'm too keen. But I decide I don't care.

Sounds good. C u at the milk bar Monday.

I almost send it like that. But I want to add more. It seems too bare compared with his cute, long text. So I add,

Oh and it's Demi here.

I press send. And then I head out of my room to find the others.

Jules is having a beer with Dad. His leather jacket rests on the back of a chair at the dining table. He is wearing jeans and a grey T-shirt with a print of Pac-Man on it. Retro cute.

But it strikes me that he's cute in a way that's too old for me. And he's not Ethan.

Jules is talking and Dad is listening. I have no idea what it's about, but Dad looks interested. As soon as he sees me, Jules switches to sign.

'Hi, D. Great to see you.'

He steps towards me and gives me a hug. What happened at the market squeezes in between us. I want it gone.

Mum waves from the door, all casual, as though Jules just happened to drop by.

'Jules was just telling us his exciting news,' she signs.

I look at Jules, waiting for the news.

'Laura and I are going overseas for two months. Central A-m-e-r-i-c-a. We're going to start in M-e-x-i-c-o and then go to C-o-s-t-a R-i-c-a.'

He finger spells all the place names slowly, even though there are signs for most of these countries, so Mum and Dad can keep up.

Laura is probably his girlfriend. Of course she is.

Jules continues with his itinerary.

'I'm going to get a drink,' I sign during a break in the naming of countries.

Mum and Dad both have a lot to say about South America. They went there on their honeymoon. They will be desperate to tell Jules about their trip to the great ruins of

Machu Picchu. I heard it about a million times before I went deaf.

I pour a drink, and stay inside the kitchen. From here, I can still see them, but no-one is paying any attention to me. They are all chatting away. It must be so much *easier* for them when they don't have to sign.

I sip my juice. My eyes are on Jules, and I think about the fight with Nadia, and how it sort of started me going all weird on Jules.

After the fight, I felt more connected with Jules than ever. He was the only one who really understood me, who made me feel like I could have a normal life. With him, I could negotiate the hearing world. Only with him.

And he was cool and cute. That didn't hurt.

When I ran back across the oval, away from Nadia and Shae, Jules was there. It felt like he was there to rescue me. I wanted Nadia and Shae to see him greeting me. I wanted them to see that *he* was happy to see me. He was happy to explain things to me. He had his leather jacket on, the one that's on the back of a chair in our dining room now, so I knew he was about to leave for the day.

'You OK?' he asked.

I flicked the tears away. 'Running. The wind,' I said lamely, and I was grateful that he didn't push it. I saw that he understood in the small furrowing of his eyebrows.

'Want to come to the market after school on Thursday?' he asked. 'We'll learn the weird fruits and veggies. Ask your parents if you can come on the bike. I'll bring a spare helmet.'

It was like an antidote, squeezing out the poison of what had happened with Nadia. Thursday, after school, on the bike. I clung to it for the next few days.

Jules had taught me lots of signs in context, so the invitation wasn't that unusual. But he didn't need to take me on his bike. I could have met him there.

Thursday afternoon came, eventually, and I was on the back of Jules' bike in the school car park, with all the gang watching us. I had my arms around Jules' waist and my legs wrapped around his. It was my first time on a motorbike, and I was a bit scared, but I trusted him. I leaned into his back as we took the corners. When we got to the market, I found myself wishing it was further away.

We walked through the market together. That's all I needed, just me and Jules. I stood close, wanting to hold onto the feeling of being on the bike with him. Jules showed me the signs for loads of less common foods. 'Dragonfruit' was the funniest. Fire from both nostrils. It isn't even that funny in English. Only in sign. Only with Jules.

When we sat down for a coffee, Jules suggested a cafe with booths. I kept thinking he could have chosen a cafe with regular chairs, but he didn't.

I sat beside him. When our coffees were served, I slid closer, so that our arms were touching from the shoulders right down to our elbows. My heart beat a little faster at the touch.

Then he looked at me. I will never forget that look. It's ironic because Jules was the one who taught me to read faces, to focus on expressions and body language. He's the one who explained how they betray people's real feelings, no matter what they say with words.

I saw Jules bite the inside of his lip. His eyes opened wider, almost imperceptibly. And then, slowly, he moved his body away from me. Only a few centimetres, but enough to show me he knew what I was doing and he wanted me to stop it.

Enough to explode my idiotic fantasy.

'D,' he began signing, and I could see him choosing his words carefully. 'Sometimes people get confused about their feelings when someone's helping them. Like a teacher or a therapist ...'

I refused to watch him sign anymore. I couldn't bear to watch him sign anymore. I got up and walked away.

Afterwards, I just pretended it hadn't happened. In the last days at my old school I acted as though I didn't need him. Or I tried to.

When I left, I thought I wouldn't have to see him again.

But that's not what I want. Not really. Jules has been a good friend. The best, really. It's just me who's been the nutbag.

Mum comes into the kitchen. Her expression is questioning, impatient, asking why I've been out here so long. I watch as she grabs a tea towel and opens the oven. When she looks inside the casserole dish, she screws up her face in a way that suggests something has gone wrong with our dinner. She adds a splash of red wine and I can see why, though I'm not much of a cook. It looks really dry.

I brace myself and walk back into the dining room behind Mum. She serves and I play waitress. Dad and Jules sit next to each other. Mum and I sit opposite.

'So, J-u-l-e-s, how is your sister?' Mum talks and signs between mouthfuls.

The casserole isn't as bad as it looks, but the direction of Mum's questioning is a worry.

'Good.' Jules talks and signs too. 'Bridge just got a promotion. She's the marketing manager of the whole state.' His signing of 'whole' is big and proud.

'She's done so well,' Mum enthuses. I roll my eyes.

It's ridiculous that she's so enthusiastic about the success of someone she doesn't know, just because that someone is deaf. But I know it will come back to me.

Jules tells us how Bridget manages at work. She can talk, so she uses a phone relay service if she needs to make calls. She speaks to an officer at the relay service, then they type the response from her clients into a textphone. Most of the time, though, her job is about developing strategies for her staff.

It's great. I'm happy for her. As much as I can be when I'VE NEVER EVEN MET HER!

But Mum is an eagle. She's been hovering over Bridget's success story. Now she goes in for the kill.

'Didn't she go to a regular school? Hasn't she always been integrated? And she was deaf from birth, wasn't she?'

Mum already knows the answers. She hardly waits for Jules to nod before she continues, but she's getting carried away and she forgets to sign and it's impossible for me to follow it all.

I get 'opportunities' and 'isolation' and 'big world' and I decide that I don't care what I'm missing.

Then Jules' hand appears in front of me. He gives me a look. It's his narrow-eyed, 'be patient' look. Now he chooses to sign without speaking. I know it's meant as a reminder to Mum. I know it's meant to include me.

'You know, going to a regular school was B's choice, but many others do well going to a deaf school. B has a friend –'

'Yes,' Mum interrupts. She's taken Jules' hint and is signing again. 'But don't you think there's more scope if you go to a regular school. More opportunities?'

She mis-signs 'opportunities'. It should be her left hand held up sideways, palm facing her. The index finger of her right should stick up and rise up behind her left hand. She has her index finger up, but it's travelling downwards. It's kind of the reverse of what she's trying to say.

I like it when Jules corrects her, showing how the sign should work.

Dad waves a hand in the air to get our attention. He's speaking. I wish I could hear him. I have a memory of his deep voice, of how his words used to sound. He always looks into my eyes when he speaks to me. So even with the moustache in the way, I get his gist.

'… different ways … successful … proud of Demi … hard decisions.' He winks at me. It's very quick and only I can see it. 'Very proud,' he repeats.

'… course … proud,' Mum says to Dad. Then she looks at me. 'Of course the choice is yours. But Jules tells me that there's a lovely new interpreter that we could maybe get full time at your regular school.'

I shake my head and tap the underside of the table

impatiently. I wish she'd just let it go. I can't believe she still hasn't given up on me going back to my old school. I try to change the subject, try to give Mum something she can grab onto.

'Stavros invited me to a party tomorrow night.'

Mum pauses. She tilts her head, and I know she's pleased. Pleased in a way she never would have been before I went to the deaf college. What average mum would be delighted to hear her teenage daughter is going to a party?

'That's great, Demi.' She's enthusiastic, but then the shadow settles back over her face. Like it's good that I got invited out with my hearing friends, but it's still not quite enough.

'But if you went back to your old school, you could see them all the time. You could stay in the mainstream.'

I wait her out. There's a break while she gets dessert, and it's back on again. Then, finally, I'm saved. It must be the phone ringing, because Mum gets up before her speech is finished. She goes into the lounge room, then appears in the doorway. Her hand is over the receiver.

'It's Felicity,' she says, with an odd look on her face.

I think it's rude to leave the table like that when we have a guest. But it's Felicity. She always seems to trump whatever else is going on. I feel that familiar rush, the rush of *unfairness*. That Mum and Flawless never seem to run out of things to talk about, while Mum and I just seem to bump against each other all the time.

Like all I've become to her is an issue she has to solve. All I've become to her is my deafness.

Mum pauses, briefly, to say goodbye to Jules. Dad shakes Jules' hand, and wishes him well for his adventures.

I walk outside with Jules. I'm carrying Mum's annoying speeches about going to a regular school. But I'm also carrying what happened at the market, and how I treated him afterwards. I don't know which baggage is heavier.

'She's just trying to take care of you,' he signs, when we stop at his bike. 'She's afraid for you, D. She can't help it – it's in her nature.'

'She's also very bossy,' I sign. 'It's in her nature.'

Jules has a great smile. Looking at Jules smiling, I remember all the times he's helped me through. I take a deep breath.

'At the market that day ...' I sign. It's horrible, remembering it. I didn't even ride home with him. I cringe as I remember how cold and distant I was afterwards. I know he didn't do anything wrong. 'I'm sorry ...'

Jules shakes his head. He grabs my hand to stop any more signing.

'Don't worry about it, D. Honestly, don't worry. You had so much to deal with. You were just a bit confused, that's all, it's no big deal.'

He has signalled the end of the conversation. It's a relief.

He lifts his bike seat and gets his keys. He sits down and puts his helmet on. I watch him turning the key in the ignition, and try to imagine the sound it makes.

There's a sliver of moon in the sky up ahead. He sees it at the same time I do, and we both sign it as we stare up to it. The sign for moon is just like it looks tonight. Thumbs and pointers start together, then separate while they trace the sliver and come back together at the end.

It's a beautiful sign. It really is.

As Jules takes off, it looks like he's clipped his bike to the moon by an invisible string.

I feel better about what happened at the market. I'm excited about going to Stavros' party. And then, there's Ethan.

The universe might not give me what I wish for, like it seems to for Jules. It doesn't want to give me back my hearing. It doesn't want to get Mum off my case.

But right now, I feel good. Hopeful that things will work out. Somehow.

chapter 18

By the time Mum drops me at Stavros's house on Friday night, I'm kind of late. Mum had been having another one of her super-long phonecalls with Flawless.

'Just text me when you're ready to come home, love,' she says.

I can tell she's noticed that there are no cars in the driveway. I wait for her to ask if Stavros's parents will be home. She doesn't. And I know why. She's just glad I'm here. She's just happy that I'm out and about, associating with my old friends. My hearing friends.

I pause for a second at Stavros's front door. I'm feeling a bit nervous. I've been to his house before. I *should* be fine. I ring the doorbell, and have to trust that it works.

'Hi, Demi!' It's Shae with Stavros behind her, his arms wrapped over her shoulders and around her front. It's hard to tell where Shae finishes and Stavros begins. It's weird, seeing them together. I didn't even know.

Shae and Stavros weave down the hallway in front of me, still attached. There is a close call with a wall. Shae lifts her bottle of Cruiser and looks at it like it's to blame for the detour.

I take the bottle she offers me, and follow them down the stairs to the basement.

It's a pretty cool room. It's really big. There's loud music playing. I know by the vibrations I can feel through my shoes, and from the way people on the dance floor are talking directly into each other's ears with cupped hands. It's good to know. In a room full of action and noise, I won't stand out.

To one side there's a pool table. In the centre there's a big modern leather couch that's replaced the worn out two-seater that used to be there. There is a couple putting it to good use. At least they have their clothes on.

Nadia's on the dance floor with Lockie. I smile as I watch them. Nadia's a jumpy dancer. An up-and-down-on-the-spot dancer. And Lockie hasn't improved much since his break-dancing that day, though now he seems to be trying for some punky overtones. Nadia sees me mid-jump, and then jumps over to me.

'Hi, hon!' she says, looking genuinely pleased to see me. 'You made it!'

I nod. I feel pretty confident to give my words a bit of volume.

'Yeah, finally,' I say. 'Mum was on the phone with Flawless for ages.'

Nadia smiles. She picks up a can from the table behind her, and takes a swig.

'And how is Misssperfection?' she asks, running the words together. It's only because I know her speech patterns that I get what she asked. She takes another swig as she waits for an answer, and it's clear she's had quite a few of them.

'She's good, I suppose,' I say.

'Of courssse she is,' Nadia says with a roll of her eyes.

I open my drink and have a sip. It's really sweet. A hand falls over my shoulder from behind me, swishing the contents of a bottle of boutique beer. I turn around. It's Rob. He's a classic hipster – thick-rimmed glasses, big hair, grey cardigan.

I wonder what Ethan wears when he's not at footy or the pool.

Rob is in the year above. I know him, but not that well.

'Hey you,' he says, as though he knows me so well he doesn't have to use my name. Which he doesn't. 'Where have you been? Why didn't you come last time?'

I assume he means that Stavros has had other parties. I didn't know there *was* a last time. It puts me off guard. Why wasn't I invited?

Rob doesn't seem to notice. He doesn't wait for an answer either. 'Geez , you look ...'

I think he's said 'awesome'. But I'm not absolutely sure. He's standing next to me, and it's hard to lip-read from this angle. His arm is still around my shoulder, hanging heavily.

Nadia waves at me with one hand as she gets pulled back onto the dance floor by Lockie.

'Do you want to dance?' Rob asks. He suddenly thinks about what he's said. 'I mean, um. *Can* you still dance?'

I'm not really sure if I can still dance. Or if I want to try in front of all these people. But I'm reassured as I look at the dance floor. There are some pretty clunky moves happening out there. And I don't really want to stand here by myself. So I nod.

It's very weird to be dancing without music, but it's actually quite fun. Rob is a pretty good dancer. And I'm doing OK too. I watch the way the others on the dance floor are moving to get the beat. Even though everyone is doing their own thing, there is a common rhythm to their movements that I can follow. Once I have a feel for it I close my eyes and let myself imagine that it's Ethan dancing opposite me.

And I let myself imagine the music. I can't hear it, but I can feel it. The vibrations are a shooting massage. I'm alone in not hearing the music, but it's like I'm creating my own song, and it has texture and rhythm. And for once I feel like I'm blending in.

I can see that people are talking, or rather yelling, as they dance. I catch little bits of what they're saying. Nadia is moaning to Shae and Stavros – who are still all over each other – about how her mum is going to pick her up soon.

Ellie is telling Nate that he should go with her somewhere. Though I don't get what time Nadia is being picked up, or the somewhere Ellie is suggesting she and Nate go, I still feel OK. I feel like I kind of know what's going on. Probably more than the others, at this point, because I'm a better lip-reader. It's only when people cup their hands to their faces to talk into others' ears that I am reminded of how much I am missing.

Then suddenly, without any warning, someone switches off the lights. I feel a flash of panic, and something inside me switches off with them.

They've had a few drinks and they've forgotten. They've forgotten that I need to see, that I can't follow their conversations and that I can't have hands cupped to my ears and messages delivered. They've forgotten that they can yell at each other, they can pass on thoughts and feelings, and they can keep on having fun while a growing sense of panic threatens to engulf me.

I keep moving. And breathing. My eyes slowly adjust to the darkness. I think the music might have been turned down, because I see lips moving without cupped hands. I see people talk to each other on the dance floor, though I have no idea, now, what they are saying to each other.

I'm locked out.

I don't want to dance anymore. I back away, towards

the couch. There are heaps of people sitting there now, lounging and chatting.

I think about switching the lights back on. But they want the lights off. And why shouldn't they? Why should they have to think about one deaf girl, when they want the romance, the ease, of darkness? I remember how much I liked chatting quietly in a darkened room. I remember how much I liked whispering with my friends.

I am suddenly, horribly aware that I can't do that anymore.

I find a space on the couch and sit down, tucking my legs up underneath me. I will be OK.

I. Will. Be. OK.

I will just wait it out. Sooner or later, someone will switch on the lights again, and then I will be part of the party again. It calms me a little to think that.

It's weird. I feel like I'm inside one of Stella's bubbles. I feel like Stella is in there with me, sitting beside me, signing, 'See? This is what they do, the hearies. They isolate you. They ignore you.'

I don't want Stella's thoughts. I try to push them away. Then I feel a shape next to me. It's Rob, sitting down on the leather couch beside me. He's talking to me but in the near darkness his mouth is moving like fish-lips. His words are indecipherable. All I can tell, from his arched eyebrows, his pause, is that he is asking me a question.

'What?' I ask, sitting up and trying to focus on his mouth as he repeats himself. It's no good.

I wriggle around on the couch. I decide to nod, hoping that what he's asked me is a yes or no question.

It seems like the wrong answer. Rob looks disappointed. He shakes his head, gets up and walks away.

I sit by myself on the couch.

Finally, the lights are switched on again.

'ThereyouareDemi!' Nadia says. I can tell she's slurring her words as she comes over to me.

Shae is with her. Shae's smile keeps changing shape, moving from grimace to grin. I wonder if she is feeling a bit sick. Each of them grabs one of my hands.

'Let'sgosomewhereandtalk,' Nadia says, and pulls me towards the stairs.

We head into the kitchen.

'It's good that we saw you at the careers expo,' Shae begins.

She leans against the kitchen bench and swipes a glass sitting there. It topples over to the ground and breaks. I find myself wincing even though I don't hear the smash. Habit, I suppose.

Shae looks surprised. Like the broken glass had nothing to do with her. She leaves the pieces where they dropped.

'Yeah,' Nadia continues. 'You know, Shaeandme ... talking. Wegottastayin contact ... you, **Dem**.'

'You can't ... stuck with those people,' Shae continues.

For a second, I wonder what she means. Shae goes on to explain.

'Like, that girl, Keeeisha?' Shae goes on, swaying so she bumps her hip into the bench. I move the other glasses back to keep them safe. 'She's, like ...'

Shae contorts her face. She puffs out her cheeks in the way that Keisha does when she's excited.

I feel like I've been slapped. Keisha has become a friend. And what's more, she's one of the nicest people I've ever met. She doesn't deserve this. I flinch, but there's more.

'What about the other girl?' Nadia joins in the massacre, and she seems to have sobered up a little. Her words are clearer, sharper. Like knives. 'The one with that plastic thing in her scalp? Eew, gross.'

She must be talking about Erica now.

'Like, you should *hear* her voice, Demi! It's so ...' Nadia brings her arms up, her elbows at right angles and makes small jerky motions. Like a robot.

'So retarded,' Shae finishes.

Shae and Nadia look at each other, then they look at me. Their expression is all concerned. Like they're *helping* me.

I should say something now. I should tell them that sign

language isn't just hand movements. It's not like Keisha's puffing her cheeks just for fun – you have to puff your cheeks for some signs, or they don't mean what you want them to.

I should say that Keisha is one of the easiest people to follow when she's signing, because she wears her emotions on her face. And because her emotions are so … pure.

And I should tell them how lucky Erica is to have a cochlear implant that works for her even if it's not perfect. And what an effort she was making to talk to them at the expo.

I am angry with my friends, but these thoughts are pumping through me. They're racing around. I'm scared that if I start telling Shae and Nadia all this I'll lose it. I am scared I'll lose it at Stavros's house. At a party.

It would be worse than when I lost it on the oval with them that day. Maybe it'll be even worse than at Northfield.

'Don't worry, Dem,' Shae says, misreading the look on my face. 'You're nothing like that.'

'No way,' Nadia agrees.

She takes a step forward, perhaps to hug me or pat me on the arm. She loses her balance. I put my arms out to stop her from falling.

Part of me wishes I'd just let her.

They're supposed to be my friends! It would be better if they were just straight-out awful, like Horse Girl. If they didn't hide their prejudices about deafness inside all this rubbish about me being different to the other deaf people. About me needing to be kept away from them.

There's an influx into the kitchen. I slip away and text my mum.

I'm not the same as these people, these people who can still hear.

And I want to go home.

chapter 19

I spend the next morning in a kind of haze, trying to figure out whether last night was a complete disaster. It's already afternoon when I log onto MSN. Nadia and Shae are online.

Shae: Last nite was awesome but now my head hurts
Nadia: mine too but it was worth it. It was cool to c u Dem. u really cut it up on the dance floor
Me: it was good to c u

My head is hurting too, but not from alcohol. It's from lurching between thoughts. I wonder if they were too drunk to even remember saying that my deaf friends are retarded.

Shae: Rob was gutted that u have a b'friend lol
Nadia: yeah, he kept on and on about it after u left
Shae: But u don't have a b'friend, do u ???

My fingers are poised above the keyboard. That must be what Rob was asking last night. That must have been the question I'd said yes to because I had no clue what he was on about. Now I feel like it was a lucky response.

It feels good to hear that Rob likes me. I am flattered. In the light of day, last night doesn't seem so bad. I danced. Part of me figures that I'll have to toughen up, have to stop being so sensitive. I can't change the world. I can't change everyone's ideas about being deaf.

But I don't want to tell Nadia and Shae about Ethan. Not yet. I just don't feel like sharing stuff with them. It's not like anyone bothered to let me know that Shae and Stavros were finally together.

Me: no

Nadia: didn't think so. Wld be so pissed if u never even told us girl!

Shae: I did the most massive vom, u should've seen it Dem

Me: oh what a shame I missed out on that!

Nadia: I saw it. It had hundreds of little bits of corn lol

We talk online for a while, to and fro about last night. None of us mentions the conversation in the kitchen.

By the time I close my laptop, I'm feeling better. I study for a couple of hours. We're doing osmosis for biology, and I'm not sure I nailed it on our test last week, so I try to wrap my head around it.

Then I decide to go for a swim. Dad is away at a work

conference, but I think I'll get a DVD on the way back from the pool anyway. Normally Dad and I watch films together. We have the same taste in movies. But maybe Mum and I can watch something together for once. God knows we could do with some time together.

I know that Ethan is away with his dad so he won't be at the pool. But for some silly reason I keep looking around, hoping he'll turn up.

It's twilight when I walk home. My favourite time of day, when the sun does a swap over with the moon. I get a DVD and some chocolate.

When I get home, no-one is there. There's a note on the whiteboard in the kitchen.

Sorry love. Had to go to Felicity's. Pizza in freezer.
Make sure you use the alert pager. Not sure when
I'll be home.
Mum xx

I can't believe it. Mum and Flawless are so selfish! They should know I don't want to be left alone at night. If they understood anything at all about being deaf, they would understand that it's scary.

There's a jumpy feeling in my heart. The light through the kitchen window is fading fast. I clip the alert pager to the waist of my tracksuit pants and press the tester button. It's my only way of knowing if the doorbell rings, or the phone. That's all I have to rely on. It seems to be working.

I could ring 000 if I needed to, but if they asked me a question I'd be lost. They'd probably think it was a prank call. You can't even text the emergency number.

I can't believe they'd do this to me.

From the kitchen door, I look into the lounge room. The beam from a car's headlights travels across the wall, like a searchlight. As if someone's looking in through the window, searching for me.

What if the driver has just pulled up into our driveway? What if he's getting out of his car? I wouldn't even know. He could be looking for a way into this house.

I'm so, so angry. How could Mum take off to Felicity's house just like that? It's not fair. It's like Flawless is the only daughter on Mum's radar. If *she* needs something, then Mum just drops everything. Including me.

There's a hollow feeling inside me, but I'm not hungry and I'm definitely not interested in frozen pizza.

I walk through the house, switching on every light. Each empty room is a reminder that they've left me here, alone, at night. Every room is a potential place for someone to hide.

My bedroom window is open. Someone could easily take

off the fly screen and climb in. Maybe they already have. Maybe they've taken down the fly screen and climbed inside and then replaced it so I wouldn't know?

I close the window and lock it, trying not to think that I might be locking them in inside with me.

Felicity can hear. And she's got Ryan. She doesn't ever have to feel like this. If she wants help with the boys, she should pay someone. She's got the money. Why does it always have to be Mum? They're probably sitting down to a yummy dinner right now, not frozen pizza. They're probably chatting, the way they do, just hanging out together, while I'm here. Alone.

I hope I'm alone.

The hallway seems longer than usual. Maybe there are footsteps behind me? Is that someone's breath I can feel on the back of my neck? I keep turning around, but he could be hiding, they could be hiding, anywhere. The curtain in the lounge room is puffed out. It could be nothing or it might be them.

She's not even Mum's real daughter.

I shock myself when I think that. I've never really thought of Felicity as a half-sister. She's always been there, and she's always just been my sister.

They've pushed me here, to this mean thought. Mum and Flawless.

I perch at the end of the couch. It's the best position for seeing what is going on in the house. It's a lookout.

I leave the DVD on the coffee table. A plastic-encased accusation.

I don't turn on the TV. I just sit there, watching and waiting in silence.

It's 11.07 p.m. when the front door opens. I have a speech prepared. I'm going to deliver it with my voice. It's not going to be about being scared to be left alone at night. I was going to include that, but there's something humiliating about having to say it. I shouldn't have to. Mum should just know.

It's going to be about me getting a DVD to watch together, and it's going to be about Mum being Felicity's slave, running over there all the time.

Mum doesn't see me straight away. I watch as her eyes do a scan of the house. As she takes in the fact that every light is on, her right hand rises to her mouth and stays there. I think I see her gulp. I think I see her get what she's put me through.

Then she sees me. She doesn't even put her handbag down. She walks over and sits next to me on the couch.

'I got a DVD for us to watch,' I say, pointing. 'It's an overnight. Too late now. What was so urgent that you had to go to Felicity's without even waiting to see if I wanted to come?'

Mum sinks into the couch. She's not normally a sink-into-the-couch kind of person. She's more of a sit-up-straight one. I don't like it.

'I'm sorry, sweetie,' she says. Up close like this, I can see that her eyes are tired. She takes a deep breath and seems to be thinking about what to say

'Dem, Felicity isn't very well.'

A strange look passes over her face. It's a sort of half frown, but with a smile on her mouth. Her eyes stay dull. 'She's ... um ... a bit under the weather at the moment.' She signs the last bit.

For I second I am worried, but the anger wins out. It's just Mum trying to distract me from being angry with her.

'Has she got the flu?' I ask curtly.

'She actually has had the flu. Now she's feeling tired. She needs me at the moment, Dem.' Mum's eyes have narrowed as she signs.

Is she suggesting that I don't need her?

Felicity has had the flu and is tired. I am deaf.

Which one of us needs her more?

I stand without another word and go to bed.

chapter 20

It's Monday and I'm supposed to be meeting Ethan after school. It's all I can think about. I worry that I won't be able to lip-read him properly this time. I worry that he'll think I sound like a retard when I talk.

In my last class for the day I start thinking I'll cancel. I draft a text to Ethan, but for some reason I just can't send it.

I pack my bag with all the books I need and put it on my back. It's really heavy. The sign for 'turtle' jumps into my head. It's one hand on top of the other, all the fingers aligned. The thumbs wag for flippers.

It's a cute sign but hardly the look I am going for. Anyway, I need to start thinking like a hearing girl.

I walk slowly towards the milk bar. I stop at the corner. I can see him. There's a whole bunch of kids there, but Ethan is taller than anyone else. A girl is hitting him with a flat palm on the chest. The same girl is now hugging him. It's like she's hitting him so that she can hug him afterwards. It happens twice before I realise who it is.

Horse Girl.

I take a step backwards. I think I might be able to slink away before he sees me. But he suddenly looks over at me, raising his arm in a wave. He walks away from the group towards me. Horse Girl's eyes follow him. My bag feels like lead. My mouth is dry as I try to return his smile.

Horse Girl's eyes are small to begin with, so when she squints at me they practically disappear. Her mouth, though, is extra large. Unfortunately, she's not that hard to lip-read, even from a distance.

'Oh ... sweet!' she says to another guy nearby. 'Ethan must be ... project for SOSE. I ... a homeless shelter.'

It takes me a minute to process, my mind perhaps refusing to follow her logic. But then it hits me.

I feel like slapping her in the face. Either that or running in the other direction. Once, I would have seriously considered the first option, but right now the latter seems to be the stronger impulse. It's only knowing how clumsy and turtle-like I would look, doing that with my heavy bag, that stops me.

Ethan turns back to Horse Girl so I can't see what he says to her, though I can see him shake his head – maybe like he doesn't know what she's on about. I hope.

Horse Girl stands with her hands on her hips, staring at us. We turn and head in the other direction. I don't look back. Ethan offers to take my bag. I've never been one of those girls who gets guys to do things for them, but it's super heavy, so in the end I let him.

We walk along the footpath, Ethan carrying both of our bags. When I sneak a look at him, I can see his mouth moving. I try to lean forward so I can see what he's saying, but it's no good from this angle.

I'd like to be able to fumble on. Even if I got half of what he was saying, I could be all right. But I've missed the main point so I'm not even getting that much. I stop walking. He does too, turning to look at me. We are standing face to face. Up close I see his green eyes are flecked with hazel. I take a deep breath.

'I can't lip-read you from the side,' I say.

I'm paranoid about how I might sound. Paranoid that those eight small words might throw him, but I don't really have a choice. He'll hear me speaking sooner or later.

'Oh, sorry!' he says. 'I should know that. I always make sure Luke can see my face.'

He puts my bag on the ground, and then hitches his own to his back and mine to his front. Then he moves in front of me and walks backwards, so he's facing me.

'I was asking what's in your bag,' he says. 'It's so heavy. I need to balance out the weight or I'll feel like a turtle.'

I feel lighter, and it's not just because he has my bag.

'It's just homework,' I say.

'You know,' he says, and then he pauses, like he's decided to stop himself from saying something.

'What?' I encourage.

'Oh, it's dumb,' he says, but his mouth and his eyes are half-smiling at something and I want to know what it is.

'What?' I ask again. His half-smile is contagious.

'You probably won't have any idea what I'm talking about,' he says.

'Try me.'

'OK, but you might think I'm weird. I'm warning you. It's just that, the first time I saw you ... swimming. You were ... lane ... next to me. And it was like ... kind of like ... in sync. Like ... arms ... kicking ... same time ...' he trails off, looking sheepish. 'Stupid, hey?'

I shake my head. I love his words. I wish, wish, wish I could hear his voice as he uttered them.

'Not stupid,' I say.

I probably shouldn't say anything else about it. I'm not sure I should let him into my mind this early. But maybe it's his worried face that spurs me on, because I keep talking before I've even thought about what I'm going to say.

'I felt it too.'

His half-smile expands. It's fully grown now. It forms two dimples on his cheeks.

'So, where do you live?' he asks me.

I tell him. He suggests we go through the botanical gardens.

Neither of us talks as we walk up a narrow pathway with rolling green hills and trees on either side. I feel unusually calm. Like the million thoughts that normally pump through my head have finally slowed and only this, being here with Ethan, really matters.

I feel his hand touch the small of my back. It's the exact spot where the needle went into my spine all that time ago, and it's strange but I almost feel like the two things are connected. It's a light touch, and it's only for a second, to get my attention, but I still feel the warmth of his hand there after he takes it away. Lingering.

He points to a turtle up ahead. We both watch as it leaves the pathway and heads down to the lake. I've been here before. I've never seen a turtle. It feels like a gift.

'What's the sign for turtle?' Ethan asks. I show him.

'That's so cool,' he says, copying me. 'So cool.'

We find a spot on the rise next to the lake. Ethan dumps the bags and we sit down. After a moment Ethan lies on his back and talks up to the sky. I lie next to him and tilt my head to the side. All I get is 'function' and 'Saturday' and I feel like he might be asking me to something. I sigh. It's too hard, and I'm starting to feel exhausted with all the lip-reading, especially from this angle when I miss so much.

I sit up and take my laptop out of my bag. I rest it on my knees and start typing.

Too hard trying to lip-read. Can we write? What were you saying?

Ethan takes the laptop and types.

Don't worry. Was talking about boring footy stuff.

I feel myself tense up. People telling me not to worry about something I've missed is one of my pet hates. But I watch as he keeps writing. There's quite a bit of glare on the screen. I have to lean across to read what he's written.

Wish I brought my camera. The light is really good today.

U a photographer?

Yeah, I guess so. I love playing with old cameras. Reckon I could get a really good shot of the lake today.

It makes me think of Stella.

I have a friend who wants to be a photographer.
For a career. She's pretty amazing.

Would love to see her stuff. Would be cool to try and
do it for a career. But mine's only a hobby. Am going to
work in the family business.

???

Dad has a chain of hardware stores. Earl's Hardware?
Wants me to manage the admin side.

I know the stores. They're all main-street businesses. Good
locations. I imagine his family must be well-off.

U reckon you'd like that? Admin?

No. lol. What about you? What do you want to do?

I reach out to take the laptop, thinking he's finished. But his
hands hover above the keyboard, and now my hands are there
too. I'm about to pull them back when he puts the laptop
down on the grass and holds my left hand with his right.

It's like the touch on the small of my back. Warm.
Like a promise.

Still holding my hand, he leans forward and types
left-handed.

I like you.

I'm deaf.

Really? No kidding?

He smiles at me, as though he really doesn't care, but I still
doubt it all. I know what a big thing it is.

What about that girl at the milk bar?

Sonya? She just likes to hit me for some reason.

Maybe so she has an excuse to hug u afterwards?
don't think she likes me. don't think she likes deaf girls.

She probably doesn't like hot girls, actually.

I laugh, and for once I don't worry about how I sound.

chapter 21

I own the week. I keep each text from Ethan. I don't want to erase any part of him, don't want to erase the way he makes me feel. Keisha asks me if anything's happened, but I change the subject. He still hasn't mentioned anything about Saturday night, but he'll have to bring it up again whenever we talk about our plans for the weekend. It's only Thursday.

I don't say anything to Mum either, though I know she'd be stoked to find out that I like a hearing boy, and that he seems to like me back. She doesn't deserve to know. She's gone to Flawless' house almost every night this week. I let her go. That's obviously what she cares about the most. Going over to her perfect daughter's house and leaving the faulty one behind. Dad and I hang at home.

English class is first up today. I get there quite early and take my seat by the door. The others straggle in. Luke sits in the centre of the back row. Keisha slides in next to him. Cam shrugs and sits on Luke's other side with Erica.

Alistair arrives, looking enthusiastic as usual. He dumps his stuff on his desk then picks up a clipping and places it on the glass screen of the camera projector next to his desk.

Stella makes her entrance. I smile at her as she passes but she doesn't reciprocate. I feel like taking back my smile. Like it was too *eager*, a bit uncool. It's weird, how different she was at the expo. Here, at school, she owns the place. She looks tired, though. Her eye make-up is smudged, as though it's left over from a party last night.

Alistair, on the other hand, looks animated. He thumps his desk to get our attention. The rhythm is 'dum dum de dum'. I think he might be trying to develop a signature method of getting our attention, like Helena's routine. I imagine them in the staff room, comparing notes. I almost feel sorry for him, trying to chase Helena's cool. He'll never catch her.

'OK, class,' he signs, 'today we are going to look at a newspaper article. We will discuss its content, and then I want each of you to draft a letter of response to the editor.'

He switches on the projector and gives us time to read the article, headed *Airline Deaf to Discrimination Claims*. It's about an airline refusing to take a group of deaf passengers on board without them buying a ticket for an interpreter.

I'm a quick reader. I'm already through the article. But desks are being thumped randomly all over the classroom as the others get the gist of what happened. It's a horrible thing to have happened. Sometimes it seems that the world is being run by Maggies and Horse Girls and people who have no idea what it means to be deaf.

I take a sideways look at Stella. Her jaw is clenched and her eyes are darting around the room, checking the others for their reactions. It's so, so intense it's almost scary.

'All right,' Alistair signs when he sees that everyone has finished reading. 'Now I want all the tables pushed to the back of the room. Bring your chairs back around in a small circle. Alistair likes the circle thing. There's a bit of mucking around as tables are pushed to the back of the room. It takes a few minutes before we are arranged in a circle. The way it happens, I'm not close to the door. I know it's crazy but it makes me feel edgy.

'OK, let's go first to your responses,' signs Alistair. 'K-e-i-s-h-a?'

Keisha leans back in her chair, lifting up the front legs.

'It's not fair,' she signs.

'Why?' Alistair signs back.

'Because we can figure things out for ourselves,' Keisha offers, looking around the circle as though Alistair should pick on someone else. She leans back further and suddenly, her chair has had enough. She goes backwards, onto the floor. She isn't hurt. She is laughing as Luke helps her up.

Alistair waits for things to settle.

'D-e-m-i, your response?'

I take a quick look out the door and then back to him.

'I think that airlines need to be educated about deafness,' I begin. 'There is really no reason why deaf people can't fly without an interpreter.'

I notice that Keisha and Luke are signing in the gap between their chairs. Adam is concentrating on his hair, making a side part with his fingers and directing his hair to stick out at right angles to his scalp. Ling seems more interested in Adam's hair than whether the group should have paid for an interpreter or not.

Stella has obviously noticed. Her feet thunder the floorboards. She looks furious. 'This is about us!' she signs, her hand movements jerky and fast. 'Don't you all get it?' she looks around the room. 'If we don't care about stuff like this, then who will?'

Adam stops the finger-combing. Keisha and Luke stop the secret signing. Everyone seems to be shrinking in their chairs. Ducking, as though Stella is firing bullets from her hands.

'This is audism!' she continues. 'It's a perfect example of discrimination from the hearing world. They think we're ...'

Here, she uses the sign for 'silly', her thumb against her temple and her fingers waving. But there's something meaner, more violent about the way she signs it. It's more like 'retarded'.

'They think we have to be told what to do and how to live,' Stella continues. 'They want to dominate us and push us down, and we just sit there and say, "OK, go ahead, I'll just chat with my friends."'

'The airline spokesperson says that it's a safety issue,' Alistair argues.

I understand that he's playing devil's advocate and I'm already thinking of arguments to counter this claim. Stella claps her hands over her face in disgust.

'That's what they say,' I sign, 'but it's actually not the truth. Deaf people can follow safety instructions. They're mostly visual anyway.'

'That's right,' Stella signs. 'It's not safety they're worrying about, it's about controlling us.' She looks around the circle. 'And you all sit there calmly, and suck it up.'

Keisha is holding up her hand. Alistair points at her.

'It really isn't fair,' Keisha signs. 'And if the airline insists we have to have an interpreter, then they should pay for the extra seat.'

Stella jumps in. A classroom of eyes leaves Keisha and lands on Stella.

Stella stares Keisha down, which is weird because Stella is usually so supportive when it comes to Keisha.

'As if they would,' she signs. 'It's all about money and control. Don't you see that?'

'I already said twice that it isn't fair,' Keisha protests.

'Yes, that's what you said,' Stella signs, 'but your attitude says something else. You've just been sitting there, mucking around with Luke. And Adam's more interested in his hair. It's like you guys don't even see what they do to us. Every day they do it. They oppress us.'

I'm staring at Stella. She's really revved up. I get why the article has pressed her buttons. It's pressed mine too. But I don't think hearing people are the oppressors. And it's annoying how she keeps on using 'they' and 'us'. Like hearing people are a different *species* or something.

Stella's signing slows down, as though she's about to make a point that needs to be clear. Understood. She stands up.

'We should all be proud to be deaf.'

Now she's lost me completely. I feel my eyebrows furrow.

What is there to be proud of? Being deaf isn't an achievement. It's a freaking disability.

I don't say anything though. For the moment, I'm just watching. Stella is on a roll. She looks at me directly, for some reason, before she continues.

'To be deaf is to be part of a culture. Are you proud of your heritage? Are you proud of being Australian, or French, or Chinese?' Stella looks at Ling, who's Chinese.

I feel like Stella is losing it. It doesn't even make sense, what she's saying.

'That's different to being deaf,' I sign. 'Those are countries you're talking about. Not –' I don't want to sign 'disabilities'. I'm pretty sure it's not only Stella who would have a problem with that. 'Not physical differences,' I finish up.

Stella has an instant response. 'They're cultures!' she signs. 'Just like we have in the deaf community. Sign is a language. Just like English or French or Chinese. We need to nurture our culture. We need to build our own society and make rules of our own. We can't trust the hearies to make rules for us.'

She's using the devil's ears for hearies again, like they're the enemy. It's not fair and it's not right, and I'm not buying it.

'Not all hearing people are out to oppress us,' I sign. 'We all have hearing friends and family who we trust.'

'Do we?' Stella signs, and the way she's looking at me is *really* annoying. Her eyebrows are raised and her eyes are hard.

'Well, I certainly do,' I sign, standing up too. 'Maybe *you* don't but it's ridiculous to generalise about hearies, just like it's ridiculous to generalise about the French, or the Chinese, or anyone.'

I feel pumped now. I've been so busy avoiding conflict, not wanting to draw attention to myself, I'd forgotten how good it feels to really debate a topic. To really express myself.

I think of Ethan, of the afternoon we had together and the texts he's sent me, and the feelings he's sparked in me that I want to continue feeling. I think of Nadia and Dad, and even Mum and Flawless. Even though I'm angry with a lot of them on some level, it's not like I've stopped loving the hearies in my life.

'Well, good luck to you,' says Stella. 'But when it comes to the crunch, we can only trust people who share our experience. We have to face the fact that we will never belong to their world, that we'll always be excluded. Do your hearing friends sign, D-e-m-i? Do they commit to understanding you? Or do you have to make all the effort to understand them?'

Suddenly it's just the two of us having this argument and I feel flushed and pissed off because she doesn't even know the people she's slamming. Because she's making this personal. I wonder if she saw Stavros's text inviting me to his party. And it's as though she knows about the lights going out. About what Nadia and Shae said in the kitchen.

'I agree with some things you've said,' I sign to Stella, 'but you take it too far and it's stupid. You can't say that everyone in the hearing world is out to get you. It's just paranoid. It doesn't even make sense. I have friends who can hear. Of course I do –'

'So do your hearing friends sign?' Stella interrupts.

'They've learnt a bit,' I reply.

'A bit,' Stella repeats, and it's like her closing argument, like she's Casey Novak, D.A, resting her case. She sits back down in her seat, which annoys me even more.

'OK, OK!' Alistair signs. He looks pleased we are having such a passionate discussion, even though it perhaps took a different direction than he expected. He glances at his watch. 'Now you can put the tables back and start your letter to the editor. You have fifteen minutes. Let's go.'

I haven't had an argument like that for a long time. Since I went deaf I've been keeping my arguments to myself. I feel like I could have expressed myself better just now. It's frustrating – my signing is still nowhere near as good as Stella's.

The writing task calms me down. I'm still writing when others start to leave the classroom for recess. I notice that Stella is going hard as well. I'm nearly finished when she appears in front of my desk. The look on her face suggests she's enjoyed going a couple of rounds with me.

'So, did you always have to sit by the door, or did that just start when you went deaf?'

I fold my arms. I didn't think anyone had really noticed. I give her a shrug. I don't really know why I started sitting near the door, why I started getting so weird about knowing where the exit is.

'Don't worry, D-e-m-i. It's pretty standard. It's actually *common* for deaf people in a hearing environment. It's so you have an escape route for when things get too difficult, right?'

I don't respond, but she's absolutely right about it being an escape route and the habit did start after I went deaf. I hadn't really paid attention to how ingrained it's become.

Stella fishes around in her laptop case. Then she hands me a piece of paper. It's an invitation.

'Saturday night,' she signs, 'we're having a party at my place. It's only people from the deaf community. Why don't you come and check it out?'

There's a challenge there, I'm sure of it. To compare parties, deaf and hearing. But Stella doesn't seem to have taken anything personally. I wish I could say the same for myself.

'I'd really like you to come,' she signs. She seems genuine.

I won't go. I'll probably be out with Ethan anyway. But there's no point in telling her that.

'Yeah, maybe,' I sign.

chapter 22

Ethan texts me on Saturday afternoon. There's a warm feeling inside my chest as I click for the message to come up.

> So yeah, can't take you along tonight. Bummer. See you tomorrow? I could pick you up and we could do something, just the two of us?

The warmth drops in temperature, bit by bit, as I read and re-read the message. *So yeah, can't take you along tonight. Bummer.*

Bummer.

And the realisation creeps in, even as I try to stop it. He can't take me along tonight because I'm deaf. He has decided it would be embarrassing to be seen with me in public, to have his friends hear my weird voice.

I realise that Ethan didn't introduce me to any of his friends at the milk bar. He walked over to me so that he wouldn't have to.

See you tomorrow? I could pick you up and we could do something, just the two of us?

That's all very convenient. He's happy to see me by myself, in private. The hot, deaf girl. Just not in public.

I can't believe it. Stella's arguments swirl around my head. Deaf people can't trust the hearies. Deaf people will always be excluded.

This is worse than just being excluded, though. I can't believe I got him so wrong. I don't reply. I won't reply, ever again.

I sit on my bed. I close my eyes and press my eyelids with my fingers, but it doesn't stop the tears. I am forced to brush them away with my thumbs, like windscreen wipers.

I don't know how long I sit there for.

Later, when there are no more tears, Mum comes in. She sits beside me, really close. She puts her arm around me and pulls me to her, like she knows something is wrong. I feel it building, like I'm going to blurt it all out, blurt out about Ethan and Nadia and Shae and everything being so confusing.

But first I just want some time with my mum's arm around me. I lean into her. She turns my head so I can see her face.

'Dem, I have to go to Felicity's again. Things are pretty bad for her, love. She's really struggling.'

Up close, Mum looks like I feel. Shattered. But I'm angry again. I *know* that Felicity will be all right. She always is. A proper mum wouldn't do this. A proper mum would see that *I'm* really struggling. I pull away.

'Come with me?' she says.

I shake my head, making a snap decision. 'I have a party to go to.' I sign it. I don't speak. 'Maybe you can drop me there on the way. If it's not too much trouble.'

Stella's house is behind a large fence, covered in vines. I open the gate. I don't know what I expected, but it wasn't this. The house sits at the end of a winding pathway, set in a garden with lots of enormous trees. There are statues dotted around the garden. They look like figures from mythology or fairy tales. I am face to face with a naked man. He is motley white. His hair is snake-like, the coils writhing around each other.

Further down the pathway is a pond. Giant goldfish swim around, poking up through the surface of the water. Hugging the side of the pond, lying on her side, is a mermaid statue. Her tail is a colourful mosaic.

I feel like I'm in a different world, and it's good because I don't want to be anywhere I know right now. I don't even really want to be me, but I can't shake that off. This will have to do.

I'm not far from the house now. The front door is wide open and a bright light shines from the hallway. There is a doorbell next to the door. I ring it, but the open door suggests that I should go in without waiting for it to be answered.

I'm halfway down the hall when a woman appears. It's pretty clear who she is. There's a heap of Stella about her. She's about the same height, although there's a bit more flesh on her, and her eyes have the same deep, dark brown intensity.

'Hi, I'm D-e-m-i,' I say and sign at the same time.

I know Stella's family is all deaf and that Stella doesn't voice, but I don't know whether her mum does. I'm hedging my bets.

'Star has told me all about you,' she signs, smiling broadly. She doesn't mouth at all, but her signing is effusive. When she makes the sign for 'star', thumb and index finger flicking into the air, it's large and generous.

'You're the new girl,' she continues. 'The smart one who is going to be a lawyer!'

I am amazed that Stella has told her mum about me at all,

let alone that I'm smart. But I'm a bit uncomfortable with the idea that I'm *going* to be a lawyer. It's pretty different to *wanting* to be one.

'Beautiful garden,' I sign. 'I like your statues.' I want to move away from the whole lawyer thing.

'Thanks,' she signs. 'I only finished the mermaid a week ago, so the fish are still getting used to her.'

'Wow,' I sign. 'Did you make them?' and this time my own signing is a bit over the top. She nods and smiles. I guess I know where Stella got her artistic genes from.

There is an explosion of light and movement as I follow Stella's mum down the hallway. The kitchen and living room are open plan, and there are people everywhere. A big light sits on the kitchen bench. It starts flashing, and it must be attached to the doorbell, because more people are coming down the hallway behind me.

A woman is sitting at the kitchen bench, signing at a laptop. She is pictured in the bottom corner of the screen, like she's making a skype video call. An interpreter fills the rest of the screen. It looks like he's relaying what the woman is signing to someone, and interpreting their responses into sign for the woman at the bench.

Looking closer I see she's ordering Thai. It's pretty cool. This house is totally set up for deafness. I think of my alert pager and my mobile. That's all I have.

Over in one corner I spot Stella. She is standing with some adults and has the familiar focused look of hers.

'Imagine if you had been out when it happened,' she is signing. 'What would J-i-l-l have done?' She doesn't wait for an answer, and it actually makes me smile. Stella is on a roll again.

'That's why we all have to lobby the state government,' she continues.

The sign for 'lobby' is one fist on top of the other, and a forward, pushing motion. Very Stella. 'It's essential that we be able to text 000. It's incredible that we can't do it in this state. The hearies expect us to play by their rules, but they won't give us access to basic services. It's a double standard. It's cruel.'

There are a couple of different ways to sign 'cruel'. It's very Stella, also, that she uses the most extreme, an index finger across the throat like a knife.

I look away from Stella and survey the room. There are pockets of people everywhere, and everyone is signing. I should be used to it from school, but this seems different. Everyone looks like they're having fun. Everyone has chosen to be here – you don't really choose to go to school. There are all ages here too, from littlies to oldies.

Part of me wishes I could be invisible, just to soak it up for a moment. It's like I am glimpsing the possibility of living in a different way. I wonder whether it would be an easier life – less choked with misunderstandings and disappointment.

I can scan the room and see conversations all around. Unless someone has their back to me I'm not locked out of anything. I can get what's going on in this room even more easily than if I was hearing and at a hearing party.

But I'm not invisible. Stella has spotted me. She waves and beckons me over.

'This is my friend, D-e-m-i,' she introduces. 'She's going to be a lawyer. Hopefully by the time she is, the emergency number issue will be sorted, but there will always be plenty to keep her busy.'

She's got it wrong in more ways than one. She's making it seem like I'm going to be a lawyer *for* the deaf rather than a lawyer who just happens to be deaf. And there's the 'going to' certainty that always bothers me.

I'm about to protest, but there's something about the way Stella looks at me that stops me. She looks proud of me. It makes me feel special, and then I realise how un-special I've been feeling, how hollow.

With a stab I think again of Ethan, and how he's ashamed of me.

'Nice,' signs one of the men, introducing himself as Peter. His smile is wide and warm. 'We need more people like you, making a difference.'

The woman reaches out a hand to shake mine. One side of her face is frozen, maybe paralysed. It looks strange when the other side smiles, because it's a lovely smile. It would have been a lovely smile if there was some symmetry left.

'I'm J-i-l-l,' she signs.

It clicks that something must have happened to Jill. It looks like maybe she's had a stroke or something. It strikes me that Jill's a real person and that things like this must happen every day.

Suddenly I'm thinking about the situation in a way that isn't like my fear of imagined intruders when Mum left me alone that night. It's real. If Peter hadn't been home with a TTY phone to call an ambulance when Jill had the stroke, who knows what might have happened. Don't the government care?

The thoughts hitch themselves to the feelings already swirling around my head. Feelings about Ethan and Mum and Flawless, but also about all the things that have happened to me because I'm deaf. It's all like a weight on my shoulders, and I can feel myself leaning closer to Stella's views.

'Come on, I'll take you around,' Stella signs, grabbing my hand.

Despite what she's been discussing, there's a lightness about Stella that I haven't seen before.

In the middle of the room Stella pauses, giving me a

chance to take everything in.

One girl, about our age, is signing to an older girl about a movie she wants to see. She's pissed off that it doesn't have closed captions so she'll have to wait for the DVD.

A group of kids, ranging in age, are sitting on beanbags playing Celebrity Heads.

Stella's mum joins us. 'It's a release for everyone when we get together,' she signs to me.

I remember learning the sign she uses for 'release'. It's usually used to talk about setting someone free, like from jail.

It makes sense to me. I know that it can be lonely out there for deaf people.

'We can get a little rowdy,' continues Stella's mum.

As if to demonstrate, I see a little girl pumping the air as she guesses who she is.

I wish it were that easy to figure out who I am.

chapter 23

I'm watching the kids get ready for a new round of Celebrity Heads. A boy with tightly wound curls is up. On his rather large forehead is the label 'Oprah'. It could be a good one, but Stella has my hand and she's pulling me outside.

There are four teenagers in a courtyard outside, sitting on a wooden bench beside a fire pit. Two boys, two girls. They jump a bit when the door slides open. There's a scramble to hide their drinks in the bushes.

When they see who it is, the drinks are rescued.

'You scared the crap out of us, Star,' one of the boys signs, grinning. He is short and buff, like he works out a lot.

Smoke from the fire makes my eyes water and explains why everyone is on the far side of the flames. Stella introduces us. Short and Buff hands us a drink each.

So P-a-u-l, you got suspended?' Stella signs to him.

Paul shakes his head, laughing. 'See?' he tells the others. 'There's more Chinese whispers in the deaf community than in the hearing.'

The others smile as Paul gets ready to fill us in. I get the impression that they've already been through this.

'I got a detention, not suspended,' Paul explains.

'What happened?' Stella asks.

Paul stands up, though the standing up version of him isn't much taller than the sitting one.

'Well,' he signs, looking around to check his audience is being attentive, 'you know how there are different types of farts? My specialties are the atom bomb and the silent-but-deadly'.

'He can clear a room in seconds,' one of the girls signs to me with a smile. I grin back at her. I am loving this. Paul's a really good storyteller. His hands are flying, but I'm getting *everything*, not just bits here and there that need piecing together.

'Normally, I know which type of fart I'm letting out,' he continues, 'but this day, there were complications. Baked beans.'

Paul has to wait for everyone to compose themselves before he continues. I laugh too, but there's a particular look on his face now. It might just be the flicker of the fire, but I think I see something else. He takes a deep breath and continues.

'So, there I was in class. History of the Roman Empire. And I thought I was letting out a couple of SBDs. But the kids who can hear said I was actually letting go of atom bombs. The teacher was not impressed, which is silly because

I'm sure the ancient Romans would have worshipped the atom bomb. Worshipped.'

The sign for 'worship' is the hands in prayer position and a couple of downward strokes. Paul holds his hands together after he's finished signing. I catch his eye, and he looks away. I can't help wondering if he's turning the story into a joke when it was really embarrassing at the time.

I glance at Stella. She's smiling, but there's something else in her expression too. I get the feeling that she's had the same thought as me.

'I got in trouble last week too.' It's the other girl signing now, the one who hasn't said anything yet. She has beautiful red-orange hair that matches the fire.

'What happened, L-o-u?' Stella asks.

'My PE teacher is really hard to lip-read. She's a mumbler. She hardly moves her mouth. You know the type?'

Five heads nod, unanimous.

'Well, she said she reminded me three times to bring my netball skirt. I thought she was just reminding me to bring my *shirt*, because I forget it all the time. So I remembered my shirt, but when I came out of the change room in my shorts, she went off.'

Lou's signing just tells the facts, but her face fills in the emotion. Her forehead is creased with a frown and her eyes are sad.

'She sent me to the principal's office,' Lou continues. 'I had to wait outside, on the bench, so everyone who walked past knew I was in trouble. When he called me in, he told me that the PE teacher thinks I disobey her on purpose. That now I have a cochlear implant, I should be able to hear her.'

Lou's eyes are welling up. Stella sits down next to her.

'It's not true,' Lou signs. 'My hearing's not that much better, even with the cochlear. I haven't had it for very long, so I haven't really learnt how to interpret sounds properly yet. Sometimes it makes it harder to figure out what's going on. But she says I'm just making up excuses.'

Lou has turned to Stella, as though Stella is the one she really wants to talk to. I understand why. Stella is weirdly perceptive sometimes. She *gets* stuff like that. It makes me think of the way she got why I sit close to the door all the time.

Stella puts her arms around Lou's shoulder.

'They're not excuses,' Stella signs. 'They're reasons.'

She looks over to me, her eyebrows raised, and I get that she's asking me to understand that her politics come from personal experiences like these – not just the big issues like having proper access to emergency services.

The others have some creative ideas about what they'd like to do to Lou's PE teacher. I watch them, but I'm not really concentrating on what they're saying. I'm thinking about the hearing people in my life.

Ethan doesn't want to be seen with me in public. My mum and my sister are too wrapped up in their own petty problems to bother with me anymore. And Nadia thinks she has to take care of me. It's made our friendship lopsided and I don't know if we can get back to the way we were before. It's all left a hole inside me.

It's weird that even though I'm mostly in the company of strangers, it doesn't feel that way. It's not that I really feel like I belong here; it's more like maybe I *could* belong here, in time. Especially if I started to think a bit more like Stella does. She seems to take on everyone's experiences of being deaf and merge them together so they become kind of *communal*. And then they make her strong. I admire that strength.

Lou is still crying. I know this stuff can really hurt. It's not so different to what happened to me at the pool that time when the woman was yelling at me. But at least Lou can talk about it with friends who understand. I wish I'd had that at my old school, rather than having everything fester inside me. It's not just about having friends who sign, it's about having friends who know the things that happen when you're deaf – and how they can make you feel.

Paul is talking the others through a torture chamber, some sharp bamboo sticks and the PE teacher's fingernails.

It's got nothing to do with torturing Lou's teacher, but I suddenly feel my own horror story surfacing. I want to tell Stella what happened at Northfield. It's a shock to suddenly want to tell someone, but I think she'll understand, and I need to let it go.

And I also want Stella to know that I *do* get it, even though I haven't been deaf for very long. That bad things have happened to me, too.

I wait until the others are about to go inside, and I ask Stella to stay.

chapter 24

Ethan texts me four times on Sunday. Each time, my heart seems to vibrate along with my phone. Each time, I delete the message without reading it. It takes willpower, but I do it. I have to keep reminding myself that the bits between us that seemed beautiful – him talking about us swimming in sync, writing to each other at the park – they're just the easy bits. The truth is much uglier.

If he's embarrassed to be seen with me in public, then he can't see me in private. It's as simple as that.

When my phone vibrates again I almost delete the message without checking who sent it.

It's Nadia.

Deng come quick. Have lost ring. Panic. Need u x

It's a very Nadia message, hurriedly written. She started calling me Deng when her old phone's predictive text kept changing Demi to Deng. It's a long-running joke of ours.

I know what Nadia's like at losing things. She got an iPod after months of nagging last year and lost it the next day.

I gave her mine so her parents wouldn't find out. It's not like I need it anymore.

I feel a bit weird about going to Nadia's. For a second I feel weirdly guilty, like maybe I'm betraying Stella.

Stella was amazing last night when I told her about Northfield. She didn't interrupt me once as I described what happened. How I went nuts in public, yelling and screaming. How all those people stared at me like I was a monkey in a zoo. I told her how embarrassed I'd been, after the fear wore off. How I stopped speaking afterwards for a whole week. At that point, she chipped in.

'It's fine not to speak, D-e-m-i. Hearing people don't have to sign, so why should deaf people have to speak?'

I wasn't so sure about that bit. You lose access to so much if you don't speak. But I let it go. I let it go, carried along by Stella's outrage.

Stella wanted to write the shopping centre a letter of complaint. But I didn't know the name of the security guard. He might not even work there anymore. Anyway, Stella was so angry for me that it felt like she was taking on some of my anger. I felt lighter.

I look at Nadia's text for a while. But I can't ignore her when she needs me.

Coming right away mafia.

I can't help smiling. In the way Demi became Deng, Nadia became mafia. It stuck. It still amuses me that the phone could link an organised crime circle to Nadia. She's one of the least organised people I know.

I catch a tram and walk from the corner. I'm a few doors down from Nadia's house when her little brother Jasper shoots past me on his bike. He does a wheelie for my benefit and stops in front of me, cutting me off.

'Hi, poo-head,' he says, and even though he's not looking directly at me, I know exactly what he's saying. There are variations in his greetings, but most of them revolve around poo.

'Hi, poo-brain,' I reply. He grins and gives me the thumbs-up, happy with our exchange, and keeps riding.

Nadia's house looks the same as it always has. The extension is at the same stage it's been ever since I've known her. There is a wooden framework on the second storey that might be completed by the time Nadia and Jasper have kids.

I knock at the door. Nadia opens it.

Without even saying hello, Nadia grabs my hand and pulls me down the hallway. When we get inside her room, she shuts the door.

'Does your mum know you've lost –' Nadia covers my mouth with her hand.

She does the sign for me to speak more quietly, and there's my answer. Nads is pretty crap at signing, but I suppose she learnt that one out of sheer necessity. I thought I *was* speaking quietly. It burns me that I still can't seem to get it right, but Nadia is all ready with pen and paper so I have to move on. Her writing is messy, but I'm used to deciphering it.

I'm freaking out. It's GOT to be somewhere in this house!!

I look at her, and see how pale she is. It was a big deal when Nadia's granddad left her the ring in his will. Other grandkids wanted it, and there were arguments that brought her to school in a rage one day and in tears the next, but she wouldn't let it go. They had a special bond, and him wanting her to have it meant the world to her.

And then it hits me. I was already deaf when all that happened. *I* looked after *her*.

Nadia's lips are trembling as she sits on her bed and writes again.

What's wrong with me? I lose everything that's important.

I sit next to her. When she looks at me, it's through the wobble of freshly formed tears.

My own throat gets lumpy, and I'm glad to have a
pen because I would sound extra weird if I tried to talk
right now.

It's OK Nads. Think back. When did u take it off?
And why?
I took it off when I had a bath last nite. Already looked
in bathroom.

We peek out of her room to check that the coast is clear.

We both search the bathroom again. Nothing. We go back
to her room.

What were u wearing before bath?
Dressing gown.
Bunny, elephant or penguin?
Elephant.

Nadia likes to rotate her dressing gowns.

I search the pockets of her elephant dressing gown.
There's nothing there except for some snotty tissues. I think
about tossing one at her. We've had plenty of snotty-tissue
fights before. But she looks too sad as she flops onto her
bed.

I point to her feet and she gets what I mean straight away.

She walks over to her wardrobe and rummages around until she finds her ugg boots.

Sure enough, the ring is stuck in a clump of fur inside one of the ugg boots. She pulls it out and holds it up for me. I expect to see her punching the air, because she's an air-puncher when things go well for her. But there's no air-punching.

She sits next to me on the bed. The tears that have been hovering start falling.

'Nads?' I ask. 'Nads, what is it?'

Nadia wipes her eyes roughly, as though she's annoyed with herself for crying. I can see she's talking, but she has her hand in front of her mouth so I can't lip-read her. I gently pull her hand away.

'I'm failing biology ... I have to sit next to sweaty Sam.'

Nadia probably wouldn't have chosen to do biology if she knew I was leaving. I've always helped her with science. I always sat next to her and explained things to get her over the line. And sweaty Sam deserves his name – he has a serious BO problem.

I'm about to tell her that I can still help her, but she keeps talking.

'... didn't think you'd ever leave ... by myself ... Shae and Stav ... together ... Tried so hard ... deaf ... I know ... mistakes though ... haven't ... enough.'

She's wiping her face with her hand as she speaks so I miss bits. But I get the gist. I know Nadia is saying she tried hard when I went deaf, and I remember the early days, right after I went deaf. She was always there, always bringing me those crappy books, always hanging out with me in my room. She *did* try. And we were always together at school.

I get that all this has been really hard on her too.

She's been lonely without me there at school.

Maybe when she promised to care for me, she didn't mean it would be a one-way street. Maybe Nadia was right when she accused me of making everything about me.

It's horrible seeing Nads so sad. I know I've been pretty down on her recently. I've criticised her. But I don't like seeing *her* down on herself.

I can think of lots of times when I missed something and Nadia told me not to worry about it. I can think of other things she's done wrong, but maybe I never really explained how these things made me feel. Not clearly enough anyway.

'What mistakes?' I ask.

'… thing with Shae … your new friends, saying they looked retarded.'

I take in a sharp breath. I didn't think she knew how offended I was by that.

'Your face dropped, like this,' she says.

She does an impression of my face dropping. It's actually

pretty funny and I feel a little snort-giggle coming out of my nose.

'Yeah, that was pretty bad Nads,' I say. 'Especially coming from my *most* retarded friend.'

There are still tears in her eyes, but her mouth curves upwards.

'Nads', I say slowly, and hope I'm not talking too loudly, 'the girl at the careers expo who you thought looked really weird with her cheeks all puffed out? Keisha? She's a great signer because she uses her face as much as she uses her hands. It makes her easy to understand. See, signing isn't all about your hands, it's about expressions and body language too. All of them work together. Do you get what I mean?'

Nadia leans back against the wall, taking in what I've said. She nods slowly.

'And the other girl, Erica,' I say. 'If she sounds a bit like a robot, it's because she's only ever heard speech that sounds a bit robotic through her cochlear. It was really brave of her to talk out loud with you guys. She was really trying, you know?'

Nadia pulls a stray bit of fluff from her ugg boot and flicks it at me. I flick it back to her.

'So, what are they like, these new ...' I can see she's struggling to find the word.

'Friends,' I finish for her. When I say that, I feel kind of shivery. I think of how I felt on my first day at the College, what I thought of all the others.

'Keisha's a real sweetie,' I begin, smiling. 'She's kind and she's funny and she's really open and a little bit kooky. She's totally in love with this guy called Luke, and she really went for it and now he likes her back.'

Nadia fluffs a pillow and puts it behind her head, like she wants to listen. Like she cares.

'What about the others?' she asks.

I tell her about Erica and Cam and some of the teachers, and finally we arrive at Stella. Nadia remembers seeing her at the careers expo.

'She looks really cool,' Nadia says. 'Is she a bit goth?'

I nod. 'She is a bit goth. She's also really smart and ambitious. She wants to be a photographer. Her pictures are amazing. They're all about what it's like to be deaf. She's really political about it. She reckons deafness is a culture and she thinks the deaf community should stick together.'

'What? And ditch everyone who can hear?' Nadia asks.

'No. Well, yes, I guess Stella does kind of think that,' I say. I don't want Nadia to know how close I've skated to the same thoughts in the past few days.

There's an uncomfortable moment as Nadia takes that in. When she speaks again, she's changed the subject.

'So how're your mum and dad? And Flawless?' she asks.

'Dad's fine,' I say. 'Mum and Flawless are like this.' I cross my fingers. 'Mum's always going over there, looking after the boys and cooking their dinner.'

Nadia tilts her head. 'Why? What's up?' she asks. 'That doesn't ... like Miss Perfection. She's normally ... under control.'

Now it's my turn to lean back against the wall and think. Nadia's right. Something *is* going on with Felicity.

'I don't know, Nads,' I admit. She's got me thinking about it, though, and I'm going to find out what's going on.

'So, ... more important ... any cute boys?' she says.

It's funny in a funny-interesting way. I didn't even think of telling Stella about Ethan and the date and his horrible text. I guess part of me thinks that Stella might say I've brought it on myself by falling for a hearing boy.

But I can tell Nads. From beginning to end.

'Maybe you missed something?' she offers, at the end of my story. 'I mean, he ... mad ... didn't want ... seen with you!'

I shake my head. 'It's just how it is,' I say, and it's nice that Nadia keeps on and on about how mad Ethan would be to lose me. It's nice that she gets carried away, telling me that any boy would be happy to go out with me. Even though she's obviously wrong about Ethan.

Nadia looks up at the door. I follow her gaze and see her

dad is standing there.

'Hello, love,' he says. He has on his favorite apron, the one that says, *Paris, London, Barcelona, Colac.* 'Stay for dinner? It's curry. Chicken. No seafood and no mushrooms.'

I smile at him. I love how he remembers what I do and don't like. I love Mr D's chicken curry. But now I've started thinking about Felicity I need to check out what's going on. Felicity and Ryan's place is only a fifteen-minute walk from Nadia's.

'Thanks,' I say to Nadia's dad, 'but I have to go.'

'OK, love. ... every Sunday, hey? Holidays ... couple of weeks.'

I'm looking forward to the school holidays, especially now that Nadia will definitely be part of them. I'm looking forward to Mr D's chicken curry too.

'I'll totally be here,' I say.

Mr D gives me a thumbs-up as he leaves the room.

When I look back at Nadia, she's gone all sooky again, like she doesn't want me to go.

'I don't want to lose you,' she says.

I point to the ring, now safely on her finger. 'You won't lose me, Nads. I just went missing for a while.'

chapter 25

Ryan answers the door, wearing a suit and tie and rubber gloves. He doesn't normally do much housework.

'Interesting look,' I say.

'Yeah ... thinking ... patent it,' he says. 'Good to see you, Dem.'

I follow him down the hallway and into the kitchen. The kitchen table is littered with documents.

'Been working ... home ... boys ... your place. Your mum's ... amazing.'

I can see into the playroom from here. There are toys all over the carpet. It's very un-Felicity. And there's always silence for me, but somehow it's more intense than usual. It's like the house is sighing a noiseless sigh, waiting for the boys to come back and stir it up.

'What's going on?' I ask.

Ryan pulls a chair out and sits down heavily, still rubber gloved.

'Stress, I guess,' he says, shrugging and looking pretty stressed himself. He frowns, like he wants to say more but doesn't know what it is he should say.

I want to turn back time, this time not just so I can hear again, but so I can see Ryan without this new frown, without the greying at his temples.

He points up the stairs with a rubber-gloved finger.

I am even more worried as I head up the stairs towards Felicity and Ryan's bedroom.

She's not asleep. She's sitting on the bed in her silky pink pyjamas. Her eyes are open, but there's a sort of vacant look in them. I pause in the doorway, not sure if she's registered I'm there. She's staring out the window. Her blonde hair is dark at the roots and she's pale. It's the first time in years I've seen her without make-up. It makes her look younger; sadder.

There are pills, reading glasses and a book lying face-down on her bedside table. I walk over and sit in the armchair by the bed. It's white leather, and I can see a child's handprint in something like Vegemite on the back of it. At least I hope it's Vegemite.

'Hi, Dem,' Felicity says as she turns to me. She points to the drawer in her bedside table. 'Too tired to sign,' she says.

I nod and take out a notepad and pen. It's a beautiful notepad with a purple and green cover. An image of Ethan in his purple footy jersey whirs through my mind. I push it out and open the notepad to the first page.

It's a virgin pad. Nothing is in it yet.

I take a deep breath. It's hard to know how to start, and I don't know whether to speak or write. But if I can't speak to my own sister without worrying about the way my voice sounds then I don't know who I can speak to.

'What's wrong, Felicity?' I ask, in what I hope is a gentle voice.

She pulls her knees up under the bedcovers. I hand her the pad and the pen. Her handwriting is almost the same as mine. I've forgotten that. I've forgotten how I used to copy her until it became my own style too.

I wanted to be a good mum, you know?
I wanted to be a better mum.

My impulse is to say that she already *is* a good mum, but I don't. I don't want to give her platitudes. It looks like she needs more than that.

'Better than who?' I ask. 'Your mum, or mine?'

Mine. Yours is unreal. A lioness, all protection and love for us both. Mine was always too busy. Used to go to hers on custody nights and she'd get a babysitter. She'd come and show me how great she looked before she left. Like I cared.

Then she'd leave a present on my bed.
New clothes, stuffed animals. Blackmail.

I watch without commenting as Felicity writes all this. It takes a little while. Felicity is not a whiner. She's never said any of this to me before, but I still feel like I should have known. I remember her mum coming to take her for custody visits. I remember thinking Vivian was really glamorous compared to my mum.

Mum is super-bossy, and she has been driving me crazy about all this school stuff. And I honestly feel like she hasn't been that interested in me lately. But I guess I do know that she cares. About Felicity. And about me.

I give it a moment for the thought to settle. I try to find a home for it inside me, and it's surprising that there seems to be a hollow part, a shape there where it might fit.

'But you're nothing like your mum,' I say. 'You're more like our mum. And you stayed home with the boys instead of finishing law, remember?'

She takes the pad.

Huh! That was the idea. But turns out I'm no better than she was. Don't have the patience. Can't even teach my son to make friends. Harry has ONE friend at school. You know that?

Had to invite Ryan's work mates over just to get some kids for his party.

It clunks inside me, this information. It's like a rock that lands in the pit of my stomach. I'd assumed that she invited those people for her own reasons.

I've been so unfair.

'Flick, you ARE a good mum.'

The nickname comes to me like I've never abandoned it. It's what I used to call her before I started thinking of her as Flawless.

'And Harry's shy, but he's gorgeous. He'll make friends in time. They're both beautiful boys.'

I know. That's why they deserve more.

'Don't be crazy. They love you and they're lucky to have you. And a mum can't *teach* her kids to make friends.'

Flick is being too hard on herself, just like Nadia was this afternoon. I feel like I've let myself off the hook somehow. I haven't been seeing the full picture, with Flick or with Mum, and I've been pretty mean, really.

Flick closes her eyes and pushes her fingers against them, her palms pressed into her cheeks. It's at least two minutes before she writes anything again.

I love them too but it's not enough. I get so frustrated. They need me ALL the time and I want to escape. I get this feeling, like they're sucking the life out of me. Like they've taken all my dreams. And then I feel guilty, like I should be happy but I'm not.

She looks around as though instructions for how to be happy are something she might find written on a piece of paper. I notice that her breathing is coming short and fast. I take hold of her hand, wondering whether I might not be the only one in the family who has panic attacks.

I wait. When she's calmed down, I gently remind her that Mum sometimes loses her temper with us, and used to a lot more when we were younger. 'No-one's patient all the time,' I say.

It takes her a while to focus back on the notepad. Finally, she writes again. She leaves a big space and then the two words she writes are larger, much larger than her others.

You are

I shake my head. 'I don't have them 24-7,' I protest. 'I can give them back!'

I pause while I think it all through. Something occurs

to me.

'Maybe you could go back to uni? Finish your course?'

Flick shakes her head and writes,

> Ryan wants me to look after the boys until they're both at school. He'd be disappointed in me. I'd be disappointed in me.

I can feel the pressure she's under, and I wonder why I've never realised this about my sister before. Maybe it's not so easy to please everyone all the time. It must be tough to cope with the stress of trying to be flawless, rather than doing what she needs to do and thinking what she needs to think.

'I doubt it,' I say. 'But even if it's true, you'd all get over it pretty quickly. No-one can be everything to everybody. No-one's perfect.'

She jabs at the words already written in the notebook.

You are

I stare at her. I can't believe she'd think that about me. It feels a long way from the truth.

'Flick, I'm not perfect. I'm deaf, in case you haven't noticed! And I've been pretty angry about it, too.'

Felicity smiles, and it's unlike any smile I've ever seen on her. It's not a perfect beam of pearly-white teeth. It's small and wistful.

I'm not sure what takes hold of me. Maybe it's because everything has been too serious, but I cross my eyes and poke out my tongue. It's a Dad gesture. I know it and Flick knows it.

I can't hear her laughter, or my own. I wish I could. But I can feel it and see it, so not being able to hear it doesn't change the experience of my sister and me, laughing until we cry.

chapter 26

I'm walking to homeroom on Monday morning when someone covers my eyes from behind. My heart jumps for a moment before I calm down. I swing around and lose the hands. It's Keisha. Luke is standing next to her.

'Hi,' I sign. 'How was your weekend?'

'Luke had a giant hangover yesterday,' Keisha signs, and the face she's making is all sympathy, like the hangover had just happened to Luke without any help from him. Typical sweet Keisha.

'What from?' I ask, not thinking.

'It was the footy function,' Luke signs. He smiles. 'Ethan looks good in a tutu.'

Luke makes the sign for 'tutu', his hands darting out from his waist to make a frou-frou skirt, and it *should* be funny. I do get a sudden image of Ethan in pink netting, but I don't want it. I take in a sharp breath.

'What about you, Chatter?' I ask. 'Did you have a hangover too?'

'I wasn't there,' Keisha replies, looking surprised.

'That would have been awkward,' Luke signs and they both laugh.

Now I'm confused. Why would it have been awkward for Luke to take Keisha along? He's deaf too, so *he* wouldn't be embarrassed by her.

'I might go next time,' Keisha signs, laughing again. 'It might be fun to crash a boys' night.'

Luke and Keisha start walking towards homeroom again. I watch as he puts his arm around her waist. His hand strays down to her bum and she pulls it back to her waist.

It's official. I. Am. An. Idiot. I have been an idiot with so many people that I reckon I need to make a list so I don't forget them all.

Flick.

Mum.

Nadia.

Ethan.

I can't believe I got this wrong too, but I've never been as happy to get something wrong as I am right now. I am a grinning idiot.

Ethan is not embarrassed by me.

I've deleted his texts without reading them. I will never know what they said. He must be wondering why I haven't replied to them. I don't know if I want to tell him, either. If he doesn't know why I've been silent, I don't want to be the one to explain. It would be like polluting him with my stupid, paranoid thoughts.

At least I can text him now. I'm going to be late for homeroom, but this is important. Really important.

> Hey Ethan. Sorry I didn't get back to u on the
> wkend. I had some family stuff to sort out.
> I hope u had fun at the footy function. Will I get
> to c the tutu??? Anyway would b good to get
> together again if u want 2. Am around most arvos
> this week, or maybe the wkend or on the hols.
> Maybe we could do some laps or maybe go 2
> the park again or whatever.

'Long text.' It's Stella and she's right beside me.

I nod, but cover the text with my hand.

'Who's it to?' she asks.

'Nobody,' I reply, a little too quickly. I know I look defensive, but that's how I feel. 'Just a friend,' I add.

Stella shrugs and walks off to homeroom.

When I press send, I'm definitely doing a Jules. I'm begging the universe for Ethan to text me back. Please.

I'm sitting with Keisha when I check my phone at lunchtime. There's a text from him.

> Good to hear from you. Hope things ok with family. Can you meet me tonight after school? Feel like it's been ages. We could go to the park, where we sat last time? I'll be the guy in the pink tutu.

'Cute,' Keisha says, looking over my shoulder. 'You two make a good couple. Like me and Luke.'

I grin at her. I'm rapt. Totally. But I told Flick I'd look after Harry and Oscar tonight. I text Ethan. His reply comes back straight away.

> Love kids. Bring them?

When I collect Harry and Oscar, Flick is out of bed, though she's still in her pyjamas. In fact, she's sitting at the kitchen table, going through some notes and bills and stuff. It looks like a baby step to somewhere better for her. I hope it is. I don't say anything about it though – Flick doesn't need the pressure.

'Are you sure this is OK, Dem?' she asks, looking at me closely.

'Totally,' I reply, and suddenly I have an armful of Oscar, and Harry is standing beside me beaming his most gorgeous smile like the world is new and exciting and he's happy that I'm taking him out.

The tram is pretty busy. I manage to get a seat for the boys, but I have to stand. As it rocks along, I'm in my own brand-new world too. A world where a gorgeous boy is waiting for me at the park. A gorgeous boy who is *not* embarrassed to be seen with a deaf girl.

There's a tap on my shoulder as we approach a stop.

'I said, excuse me!' says a young woman in a business suit, looking very unimpressed. It looks like she's been saying that for ages and thinks I've been ignoring her.

I look her in the eyes and point to my ears. 'I'm deaf,' I say, and for the first time it doesn't feel awful to say it.

It's a reason, not an excuse, and she needs to know that I haven't been rude on purpose.

Her hand flies up to her chest and her expression completely changes, like she thinks she's been a tool.

'Oh, sorry!' she says. 'Really sorry.'

I smile at her. 'It's OK,' I say. Because it is. It's OK.

Harry is holding my right hand and Oscar has my left as we walk into the park. When Oscar spots the playground equipment up ahead, he lets go of my hand and bolts over to it. Harry looks up at me for permission.

'It's OK, Haz,' I say. 'Go play.'

Harry skips over to the equipment, and I feel a little pang for him. I wonder whether it's OK for him at school, skipping around like that. I wonder whether that feeds into him not having many friends – perhaps it's not boyish enough? I know how cruel kids can be to each other. But he looks happy skipping. I'm not going to be the one to take that away.

I look around to see if Ethan's here yet. He might not see us where we are. We were supposed to meet at the top of the hill. I look up there as I push Oscar on the swing, but I can't see him.

I feel a light touch on my shoulder. It's the touch of a big, careful hand. It's the touch of a hand that doesn't want to give me a fright.

I turn around, and there he is. He must have gone home after school, because he's wearing grey skinny-leg jeans, a white T-shirt and Vans. Mmmm.

'Hi,' I say, not worrying about how my voice sounds. 'No tutu? Very disappointing.'

His smile could melt me. Especially if he keeps his hand on my shoulder.

'It wasn't pretty,' he says. 'You're lucky ... saved ...'

Ethan steps in front of me and slows down the swing. Oscar must have been calling to get off, because as soon as he can, he jumps off and runs towards the slide.

Ethan and I follow. Harry is standing inside the little house near the slide. He has gathered some tanbark in a pile. I know he's getting ready to sell me something. I'm about to explain the game when Ethan pretends to pull some money out of his pocket and hands it over to Harry. He receives a piece of tanbark in exchange and starts licking an imaginary ice-cream.

I introduce them. Harry puts his hand out for a hand-shake, and Ethan does it properly, without laughing.

Mmmm.

We stay at the playground for a while. Oscar is obsessed with a duck on a spring that rocks and rocks and rocks. It looks like he won't tire of it for a long time.

Harry taps my leg to get my attention. 'Let's play the animal game,' he says up at me.

Harry loves learning the signs for animals. I'm not so sure I want to do it right now, with Ethan, but Harry's already pulling me to sit under a big tree.

Harry pulls me around to the far side of the tree so Ethan can't see us for a moment.

'Do it little so Ethan doesn't see,' Harry says.

I make my signing small and secretive, so that it's only for Harry's eyes.

I make the sign for 'cat' and Harry copies even though he's done this sign heaps. To make sure he's got it *exactly* right. Then we re-position ourselves so that Ethan can see us properly.

The sign is basically the right hand stroking the left hand twice.

'Cat!' Ethan says.

Harry claps his hands together. Then he pulls me aside for another go.

'Make it harder,' he says. I give him snake.

Harry delivers the sign perfectly. It's the index finger and the middle finger flicking out like snake fangs in front of the mouth.

'Rabbit?' Ethan guesses.

Harry grins and shakes his head.

'Fox?' Ethan tries again. It's so cute, watching Harry crack up. It's infectious. I get the giggles as Ethan goes through a whole list of animals with big ears. He's on the wrong track totally.

'Elephant. Beetle. Mosquito.'

Each time Ethan guesses wrong Harry is more delighted.

Oscar must have finally had enough of the rocking duck, because he comes up to us when Harry is delivering the sign for the hundredth time.

'Snake,' says Oscar nonchalantly, pulling his brother over to the slide.

'Beaten by a toddler,' Ethan says.

'Yep,' I nod.

We sit down again, our backs against the tree, our legs touching. It feels good. It feels better than good.

'I've got one more for you,' I say. I stay leaning against the tree as I make the sign. I turn my head so I can see him.

'Turtle,' he says.

His mouth is close to mine. So close. It's like the moment is frozen. There are butterflies dancing in the pit of my stomach. We both make a tiny movement forwards. Our lips brush lightly, and it's weird, because it's the first time we've kissed, but it feels so right it's almost like we've done it before.

It's not like the kisses I used to dream about. It's better. It's Ethan. It's dreamy, for sure, but *he* is real. I can taste a trace of breath mints and I think he must have prepared for this and it makes me feel … special.

When I open my eyes, I'm a bit groggy. Like I've been asleep and dreaming, but in a good way. I can see the boys taking turns on the slide. They're OK. I can stay here, leaning against Ethan, leaning against the tree.

And then I see her. Her purposeful stride. Her blonde

spiky hair.

I feel like I've been sprung.

I pull away from Ethan. I get up and walk over to meet Stella.

'You left your biology homework at school. It's due tomorrow,' she signs, but she's looking over towards Ethan.

He's standing now, and walking towards the slide to check on the boys.

'Chatter told me where to find you,' she continues.

'Thanks,' I sign.

'Who's he?' Stella asks, pointing.

'E-t-h-a-n,' I sign.

I'm feeling nervy, because I think I know what's coming next.

'That's who you were texting,' she signs. It's a statement, not a question. 'He's a hearie?' she asks.

I nod. 'Want to come and meet him?' I try.

Stella shakes her head violently. She turns and starts walking away. Then she stops and comes back. 'You don't get to become a hearie again by hanging out with one, you know,' she signs. 'It doesn't happen by o-s-m-o-s-i-s.'

She spins and stalks away, doesn't even wait for my response. And anyway, I'm not sure I have one.

chapter 27

My feelings stew overnight. At first I think I'm angry, but I'm not really. It's more like frustration. There are things I need to say to Stella, things I need to sort out with her. But I don't know how I'm going to do it, or what I'm going to say.

Stella sits on the far side of the room in home group, as far from the door – and me – as she can get. She doesn't even glance in my direction. Keisha isn't here. I wish she was. I could use some of her good energy today. I could use her sticking up for me and Ethan.

English class is next. Alistair has given us a practice exam to work on. I do it for a while, but Stella's comments keep jumping into my head, interrupting my concentration. I find myself making dot points, as though I'm preparing for a debate.

When I'm done, I think about emailing them to Stella there and then. We have wireless at school. But there's something that stops me. I need to do this face-to-face. No electronics to deliver my argument.

When English finishes, I wait for her to go past me and out the door. I follow her outside.

I ghost her for a while. I'm sure she knows I'm behind her, and doesn't turn around on purpose. But eventually she does, hands on hips. It's not the most comforting of gestures, but I make myself start anyway.

'I need to talk to you,' I sign.

Stella raises her eyebrows. She drops one hand by her side but the other is still planted on her hip.

'I am not trying to become a hearie by o-s-m-o-s-i-s,' I begin. 'I like E-t-h-a-n and he likes me. Simple.'

There's a 'yeah right' look on her face, but I push on. It's funny because Stella is the person who reminded me that I can stand up for myself even if I'm deaf. Now I'm standing up to her.

'I know you have strong feelings about sticking with the deaf community. I admire that. I think you're going to be able to really make a difference because of that strength.'

I wait for Stella to respond. She doesn't give me much. Perhaps the arched eyebrows lower just a little.

'Thanks for taking me to your party. I had a great time. And it felt good talking to you about what happened at Northfield. I'd held that in for ages.'

Stella's hip hand drops down. I have to take it as encouragement, because that's all I get.

'I think I get how you feel. But I hope you can get me too. I've been deaf for less than two years. My whole family is hearing, and so are my oldest friends. These people are part of me. They're my history and they're my future. It's different for you. Not better or worse, just different. You don't have to ditch your family or friends to live entirely within the deaf community. I need to find my own way. My own balance. Do you understand?'

Stella crosses her arms. I can read her face pretty well by now. I can see that what I've signed is getting through to her on some level. I can also see her batting it away.

'Finished?' she asks.

I nod and watch Stella walk away.

The next morning, I am walking down the hallway past the staff room. The door is open and I see Helena in there with Keisha. They are sitting down. Helena has her arm around Keisha. I can tell there's something wrong.

Keisha gets up. She walks past me without even seeing me. Her eyes are puffy and bloodshot and she heads towards the bathroom.

Helena sees me standing in the hallway and comes over just as Stella walks past. She stops and joins us.

'What's wrong with Chatter?' I ask.

'You girls need to be extra nice to her today,' Helena signs.

'She always gets stressed when the holidays are coming up. It's hard for her to be the only deaf person in her little town. She feels very isolated, especially since her mum works two jobs. Keisha's home alone a lot.'

I can feel myself frowning. I can't imagine being stressed about going on holidays. I'm so looking forward to them. I wish they started this Friday instead of next Friday. Stella is standing close to me, like she's forgotten that she's avoiding me.

'It's worse this time,' Helena continues, 'because she's just lost her job.'

My hand goes to my heart without even thinking. So does Stella's. I can see she's noticed our mirrored reaction. She pulls her hand away.

Keisha comes out of the bathroom. Stella and I both follow her into the quadrangle. Luke, Erica and Cam all come over to join us, obviously sensing something's wrong.

Keisha sits on the bench and the rest of us gather around her.

'What happened with your job?' Stella signs.

Keisha lets out a deep breath, looking up at the flashing light that we're all ignoring. It's like the world is on pause because Keisha, who's normally so happy, is sad.

'The cafe has a new owner,' Keisha signs. 'He's had it closed for a week, because he's turning it into a posh restaurant.

But we were all told we would keep our jobs. Then on the weekend I got a text asking me to come in and see him. When I went in he told me that he's got too many waitresses, that he has to let me go.'

'That's terrible,' Stella signs.

But Keisha's not finished with her story.

'After that I went home and I looked in the local paper. There were waitressing jobs advertised for the restaurant. I texted the other girls I used to work with. All of them have kept their jobs. Except me.'

Luke sits beside Keisha. He puts his arms around her and kisses her on the cheek. And it's so tender, so real, that I feel like I'm going to cry.

'I don't know what to do.' Keisha's signing is small and flat, like there's nothing left inside her to fuel the movements. 'It's not just the money, it's …'

She can't finish, but I get what she wants to say. I remember how animated she looked when she told me about her job the day she and Erica went to Northfield. How she loved it.

I remember, also, Helena telling me that Keisha and her mum lived alone together, and that her mum hardly signed.

It's easy to see that it was more than just a job for Keisha. It was her link to the world back home. It gave her a sense of belonging somewhere. And it gave her something to do while her mum was working. The new restaurant owner has taken all that away from her. Not because she's no good at her job, but because she's deaf.

I look at Stella, and she's looking straight back at me. There's a hard look in her eyes, a challenge. But I don't need Stella to challenge me right now. I'm already fired up. My sadness for Keisha has morphed into anger.

'He can't get away with that,' I sign. 'No way!' Everyone nods in agreement.

Stella looks at Keisha and then back at me. There's a look in her eyes, like she's pleased that I'm as furious as she is.

She walks away a few steps, leaving the rest of the gang to comfort Keisha. Then she beckons me over.

'Do you have any ideas?' she asks.

It comes to me in an instant, what I can do about this. What I can *try* to do, at least. I just need to figure out the details.

'I'll tell you after school,' I sign.

chapter 28

Stella is there, signing with a girl from year twelve, when I get to the lockers after school. It's a while before she comes over. I feel like she's been thinking about the me-and-Ethan stuff because she doesn't look me in the eye when she signs.

'What are we going to do, D-e-m-i?' she asks.

I point out the door. 'I'll tell you while we walk,' I sign.

Stella's house is in the same direction as Flick's, and I know she walks home most days. We walk out of the school gates, and I tell her my plan.

I can feel her thawing out as I explain. I can see it in her face, and the way she's closed the distance between us as we walk. Once she's defrosted, she starts walking faster, like she's pumped. Stella is a good listener. Her eyes are glued to my hands and face, flicking between the two.

I'm about halfway through what I want to say when I stop signing. Up ahead I see Horse Girl and two of her friends walking towards us. They are three abreast, linked by the elbows as though they own the footpath. I get that woozy feeling, like something's about to happen and it won't be good. I slow down, and have a sudden urge to cross the street.

Stella sees the trio and stops walking.

'That's S-o-n-y-a,' she signs. Stella must have come across her before. 'Have you met her?'

'Unfortunately,' I sign back.

Stella straightens up beside me. All 150 centimetres of her, ready for battle. It's funny, because I really do feel like I'm standing next to a warrior, and it makes me feel stronger. By osmosis.

Stella leads as we walk again, setting the pace.

Sonya detaches her arms from the others. Up close, she's even more horsey than I thought. Her comic repertoire is obviously very small because she flails her hands about in a poor imitation of signing, just like she did at footy training.

We've stopped. The three of them, the two of us. Stella looks at me and fakes a yawn.

'Did you know you can tell a horse's age by looking at their teeth?' she signs.

As if to demonstrate, Sonya screws up her nose and bares her teeth, trying to figure out what Stella's signed. She probably understood the sign for horse. It's pretty obvious, even for people who can't sign. It's one of Harry's favourites. It's the index finger and middle finger of the right hand straddling the index finger of the left and making a galloping movement.

But she wouldn't have got the whole thing, and she looks confused. She's tried to be intimidating, but we won't play. Stella and I are both smiling as we walk around them.

When I look back, it looks like Sonya is arguing with her friends. I see them throw up their hands and walk away from her. I hope they've told her that what she did was really out of line.

I probably won't ever know what they said, but in a way it doesn't really matter. Stella has taken away my fear of confronting her. I could do it in a heartbeat. But more importantly, now I can see Sonya's not worth it. Some people are like giant boulders. You can't move them.

You just have to step past them.

As we walk along, Stella and I talk about Sonya and about Keisha's situation. I wonder if she's going to broach the subject of Ethan. She doesn't, but I can tell that she's not so angry with me anymore, and that's enough for now.

'Come with me?' I ask, when we come to the corner of Flick's street.

Stella stops walking. I can almost see the thoughts flickering through her head. She knows that my family are hearing, and she likes to avoid those kinds of situations. But this is important to her.

She doesn't sign anything. She just silently turns into Flick's street.

It's Harry's tennis night, so I know he and Ryan won't be there. Felicity takes forever to open the door. I knock one more time, so hard it hurts my knuckles. It *must* be loud enough for her to hear, even if she's in her bedroom. Maybe no-one's home.

We're just about to go when the door opens. Now I can see why it's taken so long for Flick to answer. She must have walked through the whole house this way, with Oscar's feet on her own, his little hands reaching up to hers.

Stella looks at them and back at me and I swear I can see her gulping back a giggle at the sight. I grin. It makes my heart sing. Flick is still in her pyjamas, but it seems like a part of her, the part that can get some pleasure from little Oscar, has woken up. I don't know if I'm just being stupid, but I hope what we're about to ask her might wake up another part.

'This is S-t-e-l-l-a,' I sign to Flick.

Flick has to let go of Oscar's hands to sign back. When she does, I feel proud. She's a pretty good signer, actually, and although Stella is being pretty quiet with her hands, I can see that the effort Flick's making hasn't gone unnoticed.

When Oscar signs, 'hello, play with me?' with his chubby little hands making circles in front of him to sign 'play', I can see that he's charmed her. Stella follows Oscar into the playroom, turning around to give me a little shrug and a smile as though he's so cute she has no choice.

I like it that she reckons I can handle this without her.

Flick and I have finished our cups of green tea by the time I finish telling her about Keisha. I say it all with my voice. Flick turns her face to me so I can read her lips.

'That's awful, Dem. It does sound like discrimination.'

'It's audism,' I say, and I can't help turning towards the playroom.

I get a glimpse of Stella and Oscar on all fours, racing toy cars around the playroom. When there's a mid-air crash, Stella looks up. I can see that she's registered that Flick and I are speaking rather than signing, but she just goes back to playing with Oscar.

Even though Stella wouldn't know that I've just used one of her favourite words, it feels good to say it anyway. It feels *important*, a strong word where a strong word is needed. Flick is smart. I can see that she understands what it means, though she probably has never heard of audism before.

I take a deep breath. 'So, I want to do something about it,

and I'd like your help.'

Flick nods, encouraging me to go on.

'I thought that maybe I could write a letter, a lawyer-type letter, with your help. A kind of warning to the restaurant?'

Flick twirls her ponytail as she thinks.

'I'm not sure. You're not a lawyer, and neither am I.'

'I know,' I say. 'But I'm pretty sure we'd know what to say. And you do have a couple of years of law under your belt.'

Flick taps the table. Two of her fingernails are short and unpainted, the others are long and French-manicured. The long ones are obviously fake. She stares at them for a minute, as though she's surprised this motley crew belongs to her. But when she looks back at me, she's more focused than I've seen her for ages.

'Hang on,' she says.

She walks over to the kitchen bench, picks up her mobile and dials. I presume she's calling Ryan, though I don't know what she's saying to him, because she's turned sideways. When she hangs up and turns to me, she looks determined, excited even.

She walks over to me and keeps standing as she writes, as though she doesn't want to break her momentum.

Ryan says we should go for it. We can draft a letter, and he will put it on his letterhead and sign it if he thinks it's fair. Apparently that's legal, though it might be a little shonky. But it still might not work, OK?

Just then, Oscar flies up to Flick and cuddles her legs. I get up and give her a hug too. Oscar is the meat in our sandwich. I can feel Stella looking at us from the playroom.

Flick picks Oscar up. She gives him a big kiss on the cheek and pops him back down.

'... play, little man,' I see her say. 'Auntie Demi and ... letter to write.'

chapter 29

The next day at school, Stella and I tell Keisha what we've done. We're in the quadrangle. The students mill about, signing to each other on their way to class.

'It was D's idea,' Stella concludes, pointing at me.

Chatter doesn't respond for a minute. Her hands hang by her sides, and I wonder where the real Keisha's gone. The Keisha who never stops signing. Her brown eyes do that puppy dog thing as she looks at us both. Finally, she lifts up her hands.

'Thank you,' she signs, like they're the only words left.

There's a poster for a photographic exhibition on the noticeboard in the hallway. Stella and I both look at it.

'Ethan's into photography,' I sign. 'Why don't we all go together?'

Stella shakes her head. 'I want to go alone so I can see it properly,' she signs.

I am pretty sure it's the Ethan factor that's making her say that. When I tell her I plan to take him along on Saturday, I can almost see her deciding to change her plans so she doesn't run into us. I wish I was wrong, but I'm not.

On Saturday, when I know footy will be finished, I text Ethan to see if he wants to go to the exhibition.

His texts haven't gotten any shorter.

> That would be good Dem. I've heard about it.
> Do you want me to pick you up or meet me at
> the exhibition? And after do you want to
>   a) Go and see a movie. There's a French one
>   on with subtitles. I hope that's ok. I thought
>   it might be ok. But it might not be.
>   b) Have a burger
>   c) Come back to my place for dinner and to
>   meet my olds
>   d) None of the above
> Actually delete d) you have to choose one
> of the others, ok???

Ethan has been spending a lot of time preparing for multiple choice questions in maths. I text him back.

I meet him outside the gallery. I try not to be too obvious about it, but he makes my heart race. It's like I forget how hot he is, and each time I see him it hits me all over again.

We wander around, hand in hand, and I have to remember to look at the photos and not just at Ethan. I can see they're good. They're all landscapes and ocean pictures and the lighting is interesting. But I'm not seeing what Ethan is seeing. He studies them up close, then steps back and gazes some more, like he's entering into each photo.

There's a little couch in the middle of one of the rooms in the gallery. We sit down together. He pulls a small notepad and pen out of the pocket of his hoody. He's obviously brought it with him. Specially.

Incredible stuff. The lighting and composition. You like?

I nod. 'Yep. But I don't really understand what it takes to get photos like that. Not like you do,' I say.

I look at his face, and there's a sadness there. A sort of resignation. His beautiful shoulders have slumped a little.

I reach for the pen and lean over to write on the pad sitting on Ethan's leg.

U should do photography next year.

Would be massive battle with dad. He thinks photography is a bludge.

I think about how I had to battle to get Mum to agree to me changing schools. And how it was so worth it.

'Maybe you could change his opinion. Take some great photos of his hardware stores that he could use for promos?'

Ethan grabs my hand. He squeezes it gently, like he appreciates what I've said, but there's still a look on his face that says he's doubtful whether it will work. Whether he should even try it. I slip my hand out and write again.

Some things are worth fighting for.

We go straight from the gallery to the movies. There are subtitles. But I still don't get much of what's going on. Neither does Ethan. Because we spend one hour and thirty five minutes – ninety-five whole gorgeous minutes – kissing. It's better than any movie I've ever seen.

The last week of term is very last-week-of-term-ish. Everything is ramping down, slackening off. Each morning, I check with Keisha whether there's been any word from the new restaurant owner. Every morning there hasn't.

I guess we haven't given enough time yet. I know that Flick only sent the letter by registered mail last Wednesday. We're all still hoping.

Classes have become pretty boring. We're just finishing off stuff, nothing new. Lunchtimes are boring too. Keisha and Stella keep nicking off to work on something and they're being all evasive about what it is. They both do psych so I guess it's something for that.

Finally it's Friday. My bag is stacked with chips and soft drinks for our class party this afternoon.

When I get to homeroom I see that the party has started early. Everyone is standing around, drinking soft drinks and eating junk food. Keisha is standing on a chair, doing a funny dance.

It's a victory dance, I can feel it in my bones. Something has happened.

As I walk in Helena points to me, two handed. Then her hands go to either side of her mouth as she shakes her head. Like she's impressed. Like she thinks I'm special.

I feel everyone looking at me. Then they cheer. They do it with their mouths, but mostly with their hands. Semi-circles made with fists that seem to be something more powerful than just celebration. Victory.

Keisha's chair wobbles and falls as she jumps off. She doesn't pick it up. She just charges towards me.

'I got my job back,' she signs. 'He emailed me. Said there had been a misunderstanding and my job was still there for me if I wanted it.'

Stella comes up and stands next to Keisha.

'A misunderstanding,' Stella repeats, pointed index fingers flying past each other in opposite directions and a 'yeah right' look on her face. 'One day you'll be able to deal with *misunderstandings* in the courtroom, D. I know you will.'

I breathe deeply. Breathe in the feeling. I realise that I feel powerful for the first time since I went deaf.

'Check your email when you get home,' Stella signs.

'Yeah, do,' Keisha giggles.

'Why?' I ask, but they're already moving back towards the others.

I follow them to sit over near the window where the others are gathered with Helena.

Nowhere near the door.

chapter 30

To : (daringdemi@hotmail.com)

From : Stella Hooper (starhooper@gmail.com)

Sent : Friday 2nd July

📎 1 attachment

Hi D,

This is what Keisha and I have been working on.

Keisha was your body double!

Hope it makes sense to you. And that you like it.

Love, Star and Chatter.

It's weird, but I get a pang when I see their Deaf names. I wonder if I'll ever get one. I wouldn't mind it, now.

I click on the attachment to open it.

When it loads, I'm staring into a photo. Of me?

It's the photo from my facebook page, but there's a body too and it *looks* like mine. I'm juggling two glass bubbles in the air. It's only when I enlarge the photo that I see the bubbles properly. They're not just bubbles. They're transluscent globes of the world.

There's a bracelet on one of my wrists. It's a bracelet Luke bought for Keisha.

So that's what Stella meant about Keisha being my body double.

It's awesome.

I stare at the photo for ages, taking it in.

It's a beautiful image, but it also means something beautiful. I am juggling two worlds. The hearing world and the deaf world. And I am smiling, confident, as I do it.

I know this is Stella's way of letting me know that she understands. But it's more than that. She's also accepting the way I need to do things. And she's telling me that I'm doing OK with my juggling.

It's the best gift I've ever received.

I copy the file onto my hard drive and a USB, and print it out. So I will never lose it.

I write an email to Stella and Keisha, telling them how much I love what they've done.

Then I forward the photo to Ethan.

It's not long before I get an email back from him. Loads of stuff about how good the photo is. Composition. Digital rendering. That sort of thing.

I forward his response to Stella.

I can imagine her at her computer, getting all antsy that I've shared the photo with Ethan. But I will research some arguments to give to her. Like, it's an image of me, so I own a percentage of the rights maybe. I'll come up with something.

She'll know, of course, that I'm reminding her that she and Ethan have a common interest. That they might just get along if she gives it a chance.

chapter 31

I am on holidays. I wake up at noon and I don't even know what day it is until I look at my calendar. Thursday. I love this.

My school report came in the mail yesterday. It was good. Actually, it was better than good. I feel great, like I'm heading in the right direction.

I know that entrance scores vary every year, but if I keep on going like this I've got a pretty good chance of getting into law. Maybe even at Melbourne. Even in my half-asleep, half-awake state, it's thrilling, letting that sink in.

I'm tempted to close my eyes again. I might be able to take the idea back into sleep. To make a dream around it, where I'm in a courtroom and my client is sitting next to me and I'm about to make my closing argument. I can borrow the backdrop of the courtroom from *Law and Order* to get me started. I might even put Ethan in there somewhere, give him a speaking part. His voice would be velvet and sand.

No I won't. On cue, Mum comes in and opens the blinds. She's asked the family around for lunch to celebrate my results, and Nadia's coming too.

I only have time for a shower and a quick hair-straightening session before they start to arrive.

Flick arrives with the boys and two extras. I recognise the first extra as Harry's friend from his party. Alfie. There's also a little girl with plaits, one much higher than the other.

'These are my friends,' Harry says to me. 'A-l-f-i-e and J-a-n-a.'

As he finger spells the names, his friends look fascinated and confused.

'Aunty Demi is deaf,' Harry explains, and it's odd but I swear he looks proud. 'Her ears don't work. So I'm ... your names ... her ... sign language.'

The kids look serious as they take in the information, like they're trying to figure out whether Harry's telling the truth. The little girl Jana has her head on the side as she considers me, making her lopsided plaits look even more wonky.

But when Harry skips off into the backyard, Alfie and Jana follow him to make a little skipping train.

I look up at Flick. She's not her old self. Her frilly cream top doesn't really go with her cargos, and she's wearing a pretty grotty pair of runners. It's like she's reinventing herself, and doesn't have the time or care factor to focus on looking perfect like she used to.

She tears her eyes away from the skipping kids and looks at me. She holds up two fingers. It's both the peace sign and the number two.

'Two friends,' I agree in sign, standing sideways so only Flick can see.

Nadia's dad drives her over and pops in for a drink. He's taken the day off to work on the house extension. The way he settles in suggests he's not going to get much done.

Mum chats with him for a while, and then hands him something. She positions herself behind him and looks over his shoulder. It's a moment before I realise it's my school report.

Cringeworthy.

I rescue the report from Nadia's dad, shaking my head as I give Mum my best don't-mess-with-me look. Mum just laughs, grabs the report back from me and waves it in the air.

I see it's a *proud* wave. I breathe in the feeling.

I turn away so no-one will see my grin.

Lunch is a jumble. Some bits of conversation I get, others I don't. Mum and Flick sign and stop signing. It's just the way it goes. Nads and I scoff down three pieces of Flick's quiche, all creamy and gooey. We follow it up with two slices of mudcake.

Nads and I are lying on the couch, toes to toes, complaining about our bloated tummies and arguing about whose is the biggest. Harry and his friends sit on the floor nearby, colouring in pictures of dinosaurs.

I look up when Harry taps my arm.

'Can you ... my friends ... animal game?' he asks.

I nod, hoping I can do it from a lying position. I watch my beautiful nephew as he explains the game to his friends.

'Demi ... whisper ... animal ... guess,' I get.

Jana looks doubtful about the game.

'Your aunty ... deaf. How ... whisper?'

Harry gets his little furrowed eyebrow look. He sits up straight, legs crossed like a mini yogi. His words are slow and clear.

'My aunty Demi can do *anything*,' I see him explain patiently. 'Of course she can whisper.'

Jana still looks unconvinced, like an undersized scientist who needs evidence.

'Demi can whisper,' repeats Harry. 'She just has to do it little, and like this.'

Everyone is looking at Harry as he turns sideways and makes a tiny sign for 'cat'.

'See?' Harry says. Jana and Alife nod, but Harry has one more thing to add.

'It doesn't matter if she's deaf,' he says. 'My aunty Demi can listen with her eyes, and whisper with her hands.'

author's acknowledgements

I would never have known how to begin this book without
the open welcome I received from Jo Tilley, Julie Graham,
Lynne Graham, El Mathias and the amazing students at
The Victorian College for the Deaf.

I would never have known how to continue without
the ongoing support, intelligence and lateral thinking
of Lidia Risicato from Vicdeaf, who stepped into my
wavelength so graciously.

To my editor, Hilary Rogers, who somehow always
manages to see both the bigger picture and the tiny detail,
and to the dedicated and insightful Karri Hedge.

To all of you, I whisper my thanks.

Chrissie Keighery is the author of many
successful books for young readers, including
stories in the *Go Girl* series and a novel for
young adults, *Outside In*.

Chrissie lives in St Kilda with her husband and
three children. She has spent time as a high school
English teacher, and credits this time as the reason she
started to write for children and young adults.

When she writes, Chrissie tucks herself away in a
room with shut-out blinds. She finds that she needs
a cocoon like this to dive deep inside her characters;
to bring to life the physical and emotional ups and
downs of teen life.